The BILLIONAIRE'S
Best Friend

CASSIE CROSS

Cover design by Mayhem Cover Creations

Interior formatted by

emtippettsbookdesigns.com

For the latest news on upcoming releases, please visit
CassieCross.com

This book is part of *The Billionaire's Desire* series. Reading that series prior to reading this book is recommended, but not required.

I hope you enjoy *The Billionaire's Best Friend*!

-Cassie

CHAPTER
One

*B*ecca Smith has a lifetime of ridiculous experiences under her belt to know when she's being ridiculous, and she's definitely being ridiculous. No doubt about it.

Here are the facts:

1. She's at a black-tie gala that most people in this city would kill to attend, wearing a designer gown that most women would kill to wear.

2. There's a ballroom right down the hall where waiters are serving high-quality champagne off of shiny silver trays, and members of the New York Philharmonic are playing one of the most elegant concertos she's ever heard. So elegant, in fact, that it sounds beautiful despite the toilet she hears flushing in the stall next to her.

3. In that very same ballroom, there's caviar that costs as much as she makes in a *month* just sitting out on trays for

the taking.

4. This twelve carat diamond necklace she's wearing? The one that's so valuable that it should probably only be allowed out of its case when it's accompanied by armed guards? Her best friend loaned it to her; her *best friend* trusts her enough to walk around in the thing.

5. There are gorgeous women in even more gorgeous dresses on the arms of gorgeous men milling around outside, writing checks to charities from their absurdly large bank accounts. People are out there doing *good*.

This next fact is most important, because despite facts 1 through 5?

6. Becca is hiding out in the ladies' room.

Well, she's hiding out in a stall in the ladies' room to be exact. It's nice, as far as bathroom stalls go. She's definitely never been in one quite like it, with marble walls that stretch from floor to ceiling, and a door that's an actual door—knob and everything. Actually, if she thinks about the fact that this stall is an actual room, she's going to trigger some kind of claustrophobic panic attack, so…she's definitely going to stop thinking about that.

Becca is just a girl who grew up in a farm town outside of Columbus, Ohio. Back then, she was the kind of girl who thought she was at the height of fashion in her polo shirt and (yes, she's embarrassed to admit this) denim overalls. She hadn't even stepped foot on an airplane until after she graduated college.

Point is, she's well aware of how lucky she is to be here, and how completely ridiculous it is that she walked into the benefit, saw *him*, and promptly exited stage left, right into the bathroom. She's a grown woman, and he's just some guy, and she should be able to handle being in the same room with him, right?

Becca takes a deep breath as she leans up against the door, where pristine white painted horizontal slats are pressing into her skin. She should worry about the mark they'll leave, especially considering the low-cut back in this designer dress, but she isn't worried about that at all. She's too busy just focusing on her breathing to settle the nerves in her stomach.

In.

Out.

In.

Out.

Deep, deep breaths.

The slow, steady breathing helps, too, until she's startled out of her little happy place by a knock on the door.

"Excuse me?" It's a voice she doesn't recognize, which isn't surprising considering that the only woman she knows here is Abby, and Abby doesn't even know she's at the benefit yet, much less in this particular stall. Besides, Abby would never bang on a door in the bathroom, especially if she didn't know who was behind it.

"Yeah?" Becca's voice is a little hoarse, so she clears her throat. "Yes?"

"Do you happen to have a tampon?"

Becca scrunches her brows together. *A tampon?* Her nice little moment of zen was interrupted because someone needed a tampon?

"I don't." Becca looks down at her tiny clutch and realizes that yeah, it might be hard to fit a tampon in there if she needed one. As of now, there's only room for her phone, her keys, a compact, and some lipstick. She'd be screwed if she needed a tampon too, and she wishes she could help. "I'm sorry."

With no further word from the unfortunate soul outside, Becca figures that blast back into reality was a clue that she needs to get out of this stall, compose herself, and get back outside like a grown-up would do. She opens the door and walks out to the ridiculously ornate vanity. Surprisingly, there isn't anyone else around. The seeker of the tampon must've left to continue on her quest, and Becca is grateful for the alone time. She pushes a loose strand of hair behind her ear, admiring herself in the mirror. The lighting in here is *amazing*; it's soft and makes her look positively luminous. It's the kind of lighting that women should be allowed to have with them all the time; it makes her feel beautiful and ready to conquer the world, which is just what she needs on a night like this.

She's got to get back out there. Make it quick, like ripping off a Band-Aid. Once she does, the sting will go away in relatively short order.

Approximately two seconds after she walks out of the bathroom, Becca sees Abby, who's standing by the archway that leads into the ballroom with a flute of champagne in hand, anxiously watching the entrance. She gets nervous at these events, despite having the luxury of being on the arm of her gorgeous husband. Still, crowds like this one have a tendency to make you remember where you came from. It's not anywhere any of the people in this room have been before, and it's overwhelming. Becca understands why Abby asks her to come and offer support from time to time, and she's always happy to oblige. Apart from getting to spend hours with her best friend, she gets good food and a gorgeous dress out of it too, so it's a win/win for Becca.

That's why she feels terrible that she took one look inside the ballroom and promptly fled, especially when doing that kept Abby waiting.

"You're here," Abby says, looking at Becca gratefully.

Abby is absolutely stunning; her hair falls loose across one shoulder, and the sweetheart neckline of her dress is low but tasteful. Dark blue has always been a good color on her and tonight is no exception.

"I'm here," Becca replies, leaning in and hugging her, careful not to mess up her hair or get caught on her exquisite jewelry.

"I've already lost Cole to two investors," she says, nodding toward a group of men in the ballroom. "I was afraid I was going to have to eat caviar and drink champagne all by myself."

"I'd never turn down free caviar and champagne," Becca replies, winking at her friend.

Abby grins, and not for the first time, Becca feels the full weight of how lucky she is to have this woman in her life.

"I have a suggestion," Becca says conspiratorially. "Next time you're in charge of hosting one of these benefits, you need to have it catered with burgers and fries. Don't you think it'd be a kick to see some of these people chow down on fast food?"

"I do," Abby laughs. "But something like that would probably get the Kerrigans blacklisted on the benefit circuit."

"No way. As long as Cole whips out his checkbook every time someone asks him to save baby seals or whatever, you'll be invited no matter what you do. You could probably throw a naked masquerade ball and people would come."

"Literally." Abby gets a kick out of her own joke and lets out this cute little snort that Becca can't help but laugh at.

"C'mon," Becca says, linking her arm through Abby's as she moves them out of the doorway and into the party. She takes a deep breath; she can do this. "You're making sex jokes, and that's a sign we need to get some food into you to go with that champagne."

"I'm not-" Abby stops short as they walk right into the one person that Becca had been trying to avoid. The one person she ran into the bathroom to hide from. And it's ridiculous, this reaction, because they'd only met once. They spent less time together than it took to marinate a chicken, for god's sake. But that time had meant something to Becca, and she thought it meant something to him, too.

Until he just…disappeared.

Now here he is, all tall and gorgeous and chiseled. He's looking right at her, like she's a magnet for his eyes. When he walks toward them, Becca ignores the urge to flee.

Oh well, she thinks. *Might as well get this over with.*

"Becca," he says warmly, like they had parted on good

terms. Like they had parted at all, like he hadn't run out in the middle of the night, before she even woke up. Like he'd had the decency to tell her goodbye. Maybe, like nothing ever happened at all.

"Tristan," Becca breathes, forcing a smile. "Hi."

CHAPTER
Two

Tristan's been dreading this moment for the past four months. He's avoided certain parties and galas—even some dinners with Cole and Abby—just to avoid it, but it's here and it's happening and he can't run away this time. Becca's standing in front of him, beautiful as he remembers her. He's got enough alcohol in him that he just might tell her that if he doesn't actively keep his mouth shut.

It was only a matter of time before they came face-to-face again, Abby had been determined to make sure of that. When she and Cole returned from their honeymoon, they invited Tristan over to catch up. He'd been surprised at the time that Becca wasn't there too, but he'd shrugged it off, figuring that she and Abby must've had a conversation about what an absolute dick Tristan was.

They would not have been wrong.

Just to make sure the nails had been firmly driven into the Tristan and Becca coffin so that Abby wouldn't try to fix them up again he told Abby that Becca was great, but he didn't think it would work out between the two of them.

Abby pretended like she understood, even though Tristan was certain that she didn't.

He liked Becca a lot. *Too much.* So much that he ran away from her rather than stick around long enough to eventually break her heart. He's the type of guy who isn't good at relationships, who's so used to people taking what they want from him that he forgot how to give a long time ago. Even though Tristan barely knows Becca, he knows she deserves more than that.

Still, his breath catches when he looks at her, just like it did the first time they met. She's stunningly beautiful. Looking at her actually makes his heart skip a beat, and somehow she's looking at him like she doesn't hate him. She's looking at him like he isn't the biggest asshole in the world, and Tristan figures he's got to take his wins where he can get them.

Then it suddenly hits Tristan that he's standing here gaping at Becca when he should be talking to her.

"Hi," he finally says. "It's…it's good to see you." It's kind of an asshole thing to say given the way he left things the last time he saw her, but it's the truth.

Becca grins politely at him and nods her head. She doesn't repeat the sentiment, not that Tristan expects her to. Most people usually aren't glad to see him unless they're looking for a shot to sell to a magazine or want him to use his influence, family name or bank account to make something happen for them.

Abby starts to tug Becca away, but he starts talking anyway, despite what good judgment is left in him after the two shots he took a few minutes ago.

"How are you?" he asks. The decent thing to do would be to let Abby lead Becca away, but Tristan's never been one to do the decent thing. He wants to keep talking to her, almost *needs* it. He's not sure why.

"I'm well, thank you for asking." Becca's tone is clipped but still so incredibly polite. So much more than he deserves. "How are you?" she asks with more careful politeness.

Tristan takes a deep breath, lets his gaze travel along the curves of her body, the way the neckline of her dress hugs her cleavage. The red pops against her creamy white skin, and he wants to put his mouth right *there*. He wonders if she tastes as good as he remembers. The growing buzz he's feeling makes him think it might be a good idea to see if she'd let him find out. Instead, he answers her question.

"I'm good, thanks."

"We better go," Abby says politely, and it's probably best that he doesn't get the chance to continue his train of thought. Nothing good would ever come from that anyway.

Abby gives Tristan *the look* that amounts to 'behave yourself, don't embarrass me, please learn to be a better person' and Tristan feels a brush of shame when she turns away. He's a fuck up, Abby knows that. For some reason, she loves him anyway. Apart from Cole and occasionally Tristan's mother, not too many other people in his life do. Not for the right reasons, anyway.

"It was good to see you, Becca," Tristan says. He sounds kind of like an asshole, but it's too late to change that now.

"Thanks a lot," Abby replies teasingly, trying to break the tension.

"You know it's always a given that I'm glad to see you, Ab." Tristan offers her a playful wink, but he's not sure it comes off right.

Becca gives him a tight smile as she turns and follows her best friend, and Tristan watches her leave. It's better this way.

When Becca and Abby disappear into the crowd, Tristan spots a waiter carrying a tray of champagne and grabs a flute as he passes by. Tristan almost has the rim of the glass to his lips when Cole walks up and pulls it out of his hands.

"What?" Tristan asks, trying for playful but mostly sounding annoyed.

"Don't," Cole replies. On most people that word might sound like judgment, but not on Cole.

"Don't what?" Tristan plays dumb. "You got a flask of the hard stuff hidden in your sock?"

Cole gives him a hard, appraising look. After countless years of friendship, such a look rankles Tristan. It makes him straighten his shoulders to fight against the discomfort of such a shrewd gaze coming from someone like Cole Kerrigan.

"Don't do what you do." Cole's voice is friendly enough. He slides his right hand in his pocket as he takes a sip of what was once Tristan's champagne, then scans the room like they're having some casual conversation, not a near confrontation.

"What exactly do I do?" Tristan's not being facetious so much as he's genuinely curious. He has a ton of problematic behaviors, so Cole could be talking about pretty much anything.

Cole sighs. "Don't get drunk and fuck some girl whose name you won't remember in the morning."

Tristan thinks about denying that he was going to do just that, but it's pointless. Instead he just laughs, because it's ridiculous how well Cole knows him. When another waiter with a tray full of champagne walks buy, Tristan grabs another flute, and this time Cole doesn't try to stop him. He downs it all in one long, burning gulp.

"That's who I am, Cole," Tristan says.

"No, it's not." Cole claps him on the shoulder. "It's who you're choosing to be."

That reply strikes a nerve deep inside Tristan, making anger flare up hot and fast. "What, you're married now, so you think you're the authority on adult behavior? Is that what this is?"

Cole smirks and shakes his head. "You're twenty-eight, Tristan. It's time to start thinking about getting serious with your life. This shit was fun when we were younger, but-"

"You sound like my father." Even though Tristan knows it's not a good idea to fight and drink, he snags another flute of champagne and downs it, then lets his eyes roam the room, looking for the open bar. Once Cole's done with his lecture, Tristan's making a beeline right there.

"Your father's right. Trust funds don't last forever, and you can't keep living like this."

Tristan remembers that Cole walked up just as Abby and Becca were walking away, and a metaphorical lightbulb flicks on in his brain. "Is this because of Becca?" he asks angrily. Because he's going to be damned if they're going to keep pushing a relationship between the two of them on him. It's not fair to Becca. At all.

"What?"

Tristan can tell that Cole is genuinely confused, so he guesses the timing of this confrontation is purely coincidence. That doesn't make him feel any better about it.

"No," Cole replies. "Look, I don't know what happened between you two-"

"Nothing happened." It's the truth, but yet it feels like a lie.

"It's not about Becca."

Tristan takes a deep breath, exhaling slowly as he closes his eyes. He reaches up and pinches the bridge of his nose, hoping that might alleviate some of the tension he's feeling, but it's mostly unsuccessful. "Look, just go write your checks. Be charitable Cole Kerrigan, okay? Just…let me be."

Cole gives Tristan a long-suffering look, but he does walk back into the crowd, probably to go find his wife. If Tristan feels a little twinge of jealousy there, he ignores it; he's good at that. What he's also good at is playing his part: the handsome, unpredictable, fun-loving playboy. It's a familiar, comfortable role to slip into, much easier than being the mature, responsible businessman that his father and Cole want him to be. They keep telling him that he needs to get serious with his life, and, well, if he ever let himself think about that, maybe he'd realize they're right. Maybe part of him even wants that, even though the fear of failure is so great.

What if he tries and fails? What if he takes the helm of his family's company like his father wants him to and he runs it into the ground? What if he doesn't live up to their expectations? What makes his life comfortable now is that he knows what his family and friends expect of him. They know that he'll get drunk and take a woman home. Maybe he'll even punch a paparazzo and make the news. Being stupid and impulsive is what Tristan does best.

There's time for introspection, and maybe Tristan needs to do that. Maybe he needs to take a long, hard look at himself and just…figure things out. As he walks up to the bar and asks for a whiskey, neat, he knows that tonight isn't that night. With a drink in his hand, he pushes down all the doubts, swallows every single word Cole said to him.

He turns his head and scans the crowd. Tonight, he wants a brunette.

CHAPTER
Three

*B*ecca's cell phone rings at quarter past six, pulling her out of the mountain of work she's been entrenched in for the past few hours. Her eyes are aching, it seems like the first time she's looked at anything that isn't a computer screen in a really long time. It's a welcome break, and she smiles when she sees Abby's name and picture lighting up the screen.

"Hey, Abs," Becca says.

"Hey!"

There's something about Abby's voice that de-stresses Becca. It's an effect that Abby's always had on her ever since they met. Everything about her friend is just so soothing, and a friendly hello is the perfect thing to hear when you're stressed out beyond belief.

"How are you?" Abby asks. She sounds a little tentative,

and even though Becca's curious about what could possibly make her sound like that, she doesn't ask.

"I can't complain." As Becca speaks, she stifles a yawn, then rubs at her tired eyes. "You called at a great time."

"The time when you're so exhausted you can't see straight?"

"Yeah, that's about the time I'm talking about," Becca replies, laughing.

"You're exhausted and overworked, and I think I know the perfect cure for that."

"Would that cure begin with greasy cheeseburger and end with french fries?"

Abby's soft giggle carries across the line. "Close. It begins with greasy cheeseburger and ends with milkshakes as big as our heads. The fries are somewhere in between."

Becca actually moans. She'd do a lot of things for a cheeseburger and a milkshake right now. "They're in an important place in between. We can't forget about them ever."

"We would never," Abby replies solemnly. "So, what do you say? Diner in an hour? It's been a while since I've been to my favorite spot."

"I thought our favorite spot was now your favorite spot with your husband?" Becca's not bitter about that at all. No, not even a little.

"You were my first date at that diner, Becks," Abby replies. "It'll always be special for that reason alone."

Becca grins as she looks at the clock on her computer. "I can do an hour."

"Perfect. See you soon."

When Abby hangs up, one of Becca's coworkers, Tiffany, stops in the doorway that leads to Becca's office and leans back on the doorframe. "Working late tonight, I see," she says with a knowing lilt in her voice. "Making up for leaving early yesterday?"

Tiffany's leading her into something, Becca knows this. She reaches over and grabs a picture frame off of the bookshelf next to the door, and runs her finger along the edges.

"Is this your mom?" Tiffany asks.

Tiffany knows that's Becca's mom, she's seen her before.

"Do you ever stop being nosy as hell?" Becca asks as she clicks her mouse a few times to shut down her computer. She figures now's as good a time as any to get the hell out of here, especially if Tiffany's going to start playing 20 Questions. If she leaves the computer on, she knows she'll wind up getting distracted by work. Then she'll be late to the diner, and Abby would never let her hear the end of that.

"Never," Tiffany replies, placing the picture frame back on the bookcase. "My nosiness is one of the things you love most about me."

Becca can't argue with her there. Tiffany is boisterous, loud, and the office's biggest gossip, which pretty much makes her one of Becca's favorite people.

"I saw a pic of you from last night. It was a crowd shot. You looked good." Tiffany pulls her phone out of her pocket and swipes across the screen a few times before holding the phone out in front of her.

Becca hasn't actually gone looking for pictures from last

17

night, so this is the first one she's seeing. When she reaches out and takes Tiffany's phone so she can get a closer look at this picture, Tiffany willingly hands it over. Becca thinks she really does look good. Amazing, even. She makes note of the site's URL so she can save a copy of this picture when she gets home.

"There are more," Tiffany says. "Just swipe to the left."

Becca does just that. There are more of the same group of people. Random people she was introduced to but who she can't remember the name of, and Cole and Abby looking like two lovesick fools. In the next picture she spots Tristan standing in the top right corner with a brunette on his arm, tossing back what does not appear to be his first drink of the night.

Disappointed, Becca taps the lock button on the phone and hands it back to Tiffany.

"I want to borrow that dress."

Becca would let another woman wear that beautiful dress over her dead body. Instead of telling Tiffany that, she says, "That dress was actually really comfortable. It had pockets, but they didn't make my hips look bulky or anything."

"Next time you go to one of these things you need to take a date. When you look that good, arm candy is required."

"That is so not the place to find arm candy," Becca replies with a laugh.

"Why not?"

"Oh, Tiff," Becca tuts, shaking her head. "You innocent little bird. Most of these men aren't dating material. They're rich and handsome, sure. But you're looking at a sea full of men with outrageous expectations and even more outrageous mommy issues, and trust me, you don't want to set sail on it." Becca pulls her computer off its docking station and slides it into her tote bag. "Maybe one day I'll see if I can snag you an invite so you can see for yourself."

"Will it come with a free dress?"

This chick is always working an angle. Honestly, Becca really digs that. "It depends on what you bribe me with."

Amidst the hustle and bustle of their favorite hole-in-the-wall diner, two friends sit together in their favorite booth, sharing their favorite greasy food.

Abby steals one of Becca's french fries and swirls it in the mountain of ketchup sitting along the edge of her plate.

"I just wanted to tell you, again," Abby says.

Becca knows where this thought is headed, so she's going to stop it right in its tracks. "Don't apologize, Abs. Please."

"I didn't know he was going to be there."

Becca shrugs. "I was being ridiculous that night, I know that. It's not like I could avoid him forever, and I honestly wasn't intending to. It's not like we had a thing, or-"

Abby gives her a very shrewd look. "Beck. Come on."

"What? We didn't. It was a day at your wedding; it's not like we had sex or anything." They *almost* had sex, but Tristan backed off. They'd kissed a lot. They'd touched. A *lot*. But Tristan told her he wanted to take things slow, and then he took off before she woke up the next morning. Becca's not a genius or anything, but it doesn't take one to realize that for a guy who's basically famous for having a different girl on his arm every night, begging off the way Tristan did, by, you know, *disappearing*, is a pretty big indicator that he's just not that into her. It's fine, it's not the first time Becca's had to deal with something like this. It's just a little awkward because she *was* into him and was disappointed (to say the least) by the way things worked out, and it's just awkward because her friends are his friends and they're going to have to be around each other sometimes now. Becca just needs to find a way past it, and seeing him last night really helped. Seeing him on Tiffany's cell phone with his arm draped around some other woman helped even more.

"There was something there," Abby says, because she just refuses to let things go when she should.

"I thought so," Becca says before popping a fry in her mouth. "It was nice, being with him. I felt…I don't know, a kinship, I guess. Close to him in a way I hadn't ever felt with someone before, certainly not that quickly. I thought he felt it too." She remembers the way it felt, sitting with him on the beach, wrapped in his arms. She also remembers waking up the next morning, and seeing an empty spot in the driveway where his car was parked the night before.

She remembers the sinking, lonely feeling of realizing she felt such a deep connection to someone who didn't feel one to her. "Besides, he'd end up leaving, you know? He left the once, I…I don't know, I'd be expecting it."

"He just needs to grow up a bit," Abby says with a sigh.

"I thought being with someone like you could help him do that."

"I'm pretty sure his BFF Jack Daniels is hindering him in that area."

Abby takes a deep breath.

"I don't have to avoid him forever, Abby. Invite me to benefits he's going to be at, invite me to dinner at your house when he's going to be there. We're probably going to be your kids' godparents, so…I've got to get used to it," Becca says with a teasing lilt in her voice.

"As if I'd leave a child of mine with Tristan," Abby replies as she rolls her eyes. But then Becca manages to get a smile out of her, and that makes her happy enough to want to move the conversation along.

"Can we talk about something else now? How's the shop?"

Abby's eyes light up. "It's great! I met with the interior designer yesterday, she brought over some really pretty colors for the walls and counters. I've been trying out some new recipes."

"New recipes?" Becca whines. "Oh, I miss the days when I was your designated taste tester."

Abby reaches into her bag and pulls out a pink box wrapped with a crisp white bow, then slides the box across the table until it's right in front of Becca. "Those days aren't over, my friend."

"I love you," Becca says, eagerly pulling at the end of the bow until it unravels. "Who needs a man when I have chocolate?"

CHAPTER
Four

*T*ristan sits in his father's opulent office on the fiftieth floor of one of the nicest buildings in the city, looking out at the New York skyline. His father, Clay Blackwell, is droning on about some merger that Tristan knows absolutely nothing about. He's completely zoned out, not paying attention to a word his father is saying, and he hasn't been paying attention since the beginning of this meeting. If he's honest with himself, he stopped paying attention when he was around his father way before he walked into the building this afternoon.

The only reason he's sitting here today is because his father insists on it. This isn't the first meeting he's sat in on and zoned out of, and it won't be the last. One day, Clay Blackwell insists that Tristan is going to take over his company. Problem is, Clay Blackwell has never once asked

Tristan if that's something that he wants to do, and that makes Tristan increasingly angry.

Despite the fact that this company has been his legacy ever since he was a child—before then, probably, when his father only dreamed about having a son—Tristan has never wanted this for himself. The thought of having a Fortune 500 company and all its employees and their families dependent on his decision-making abilities makes this unrelenting weight settle on Tristan's chest every time he thinks about it. Tristan is afraid to tell his father this, is fearful of feeling the full weight of his disappointment when he finds out that his only child doesn't want the legacy he built to leave him. Tristan's spent most of his life playing the part - he went to the Ivy League college his father paid to get him into, he took all the classes his father insisted upon and did a passable job of completing them, hoping for one ounce of his father's approval.

He hasn't gotten any of that approval in the six years since he graduated, and he isn't hopeful to get that approval anytime soon. He knows he'll never get it if he tells his father how he really feels, so he's being kind of a chicken shit by letting his attitude express that for him. He hopes that if Clay picks up on his disinterest on his own, he'll be spared the burden of having to have this conversation. That strategy hasn't worked very well thus far.

So, there's this deep, abiding bitterness that Tristan feels every time he walks into this office and takes his place in the wingback leather chair across from the identical one that his father sits on like a throne. Clay Blackwell, ruler of everything and everyone, to hell with anyone who doesn't go along with him and his plans.

"Tristan!" Clay says loudly, slamming his fist against his desk. "Pay attention for Christ's sake. Pretend you're not completely oblivious. Pretend like you give a shit."

"I am pretending, Dad," Tristan says snidely, enjoying the fire that lights up his father's eyes. "I guess I'm not doing so well? Maybe you should've paid for me to major in drama in college."

There's an odd satisfaction that accompanies the look of rage on Clay's face, and Tristan knows he's an asshole for feeling it. His mother would be upset seeing him act this way toward his father, but he can't help himself today. He *should,* but he can't.

When the call is over, Clay stands and walks over to the chair Tristan's practically slumped in, then lowers himself to Tristan's eye level and plants his hands on the arms of the chair. Tristan schools his face into practiced indifference, maybe even a cocky little amused smile. Just a little one. Clay's green eyes are bright with anger. Behind the anger, if Tristan *really* looks, he sees the disappointment there. That disappointment almost makes Tristan cringe.

"God damn it," Clay grits out, his voice hard and rough. His grip on the chair makes the expensive leather creak. "When are you going to get serious? When are you going to stop expecting everything in your life to be handed to you? You live off your goddamn trust fund like you're the king of the world. What are you going to do when that money runs out? You have no skills, Tristan. You have no ambition.

You're basically unemployable."

Tristan laughs, and it's an ugly, unpleasant sound. "And you want me to run the company, why? If I don't have any skills or ambition, and I'm unemployable, then why in the *fuck* do you want to employ me?"

This must be the last straw for Clay, because he reaches forward and wraps his fingers around the lapels of Tristan's suit and pulls him up out of his chair. Tristan laughs, actually *laughs*, and his father is so dumbstruck that he pulls away.

"You've been drinking," Clay spits, smelling the faint hint of liquor on his son's breath. "I should've known." He walks to the other side of the room and then turns, attempting to level Tristan with a glare. "This isn't how I raised you."

"You didn't raise me, a nanny did. The only time you could be bothered to show me any kind of love or attention was when my grades were good enough, or when-"

"When you showed up drunk at school? Or when I got called in to the headmaster's office for one of your stupid pranks? That was the kind of attention you wanted from me, and that was the kind of attention I gave you. If you wanted me to love you, you should've been a better son."

Tristan knows his father regrets those words the second he says them; it's written all over his face. But they're out there, and Tristan knows there's a kernel of truth in there, much as it hurts to realize. His father wants a certain kind of heir, and Tristan will never be that.

He really wishes he had a drink to chase away this disgusting, useless feeling that always wells up inside of him whenever he's on the receiving end of his father's immense disappointment. Sometimes that feeling seems like it's been living in him for most of his life. He wants the sweet oblivion that he finds in the bottom of a shot glass. He wants to lose himself in a beautiful woman or two, just long enough to forget his own name and all the bullshit that comes along with it.

What Tristan needs is to get away from here. Now. So, instead of fighting (which is his first instinct), he stands and buttons his suit jacket, then gives his father a smile he's perfected over the years, one that hides just how much Clay's disappointment cuts Tristan to the core.

"It's been pleasant as always, Dad," Tristan says.

Clay shoots him a steely look that betrays nothing.

Tristan walks toward the door, then pauses and turns with his hand on the handle. "I suppose I'll see you at Sunday dinner, where we'll play nice for Mom and I'll pretend I don't think you're the world's worst father, and you'll pretend you don't think I'm the world's worst son?"

Clay walks over to his desk and presses his palms against the surface, then leans forward and looks down so he doesn't have to look Tristan in the eye.

With a bitter laugh, Tristan says, "Yeah. That's what I thought."

He opens the door and takes a deep breath, convinces himself that he doesn't care about anything that happened here today. Not the meeting, and certainly not the fight he had with his father. He doesn't care what his father thinks. He doesn't care what anyone thinks.

He doesn't care, he doesn't care, he doesn't care. He

repeats this thought over and over again until he thinks he might believe it.

Tristan gives Clay's assistant a winning smile. Her name is Sylvie, and he's known her since he was a child. He's pretty sure she's the one who purchased most of the Christmas and birthday presents he's received since he was five years old.

"Tristan," she says warmly as she stands and gives him a hug.

It's nice, he thinks, that she's happy to see him.

"How's your father?"

"You know, he's…him."

When Sylvie pulls away, her lips turn up in a sad smile, and she gently gives his forearms a squeeze. Tristan knows that she sees what he's so desperately trying to hide from everyone.

He cares.

He cares a lot.

In a bar across the street from Blackwell Technologies, Tristan drinks away most of his anger and pain. Now all he feels is a dull ache in his belly, some tangle of nerves and disappointment and unsolved problems that he doesn't think he'll ever figure out how to unravel.

He buys rounds for the sad sacks around him. He's useless, but his money's always good. Some people think his money is the best thing about him. When he orders his next drink, the bartender gives him a cup of coffee instead. It's complete bullshit.

What time is it? Tristan looks at his watch, but the numbers are a little too blurry. He pulls out his phone, notices it's only 8:30. It's still early, and he's already on his way to being piss drunk.

"Want me to call someone to pick you up, man?" The bartender says, shooting him a look that comes off a whole hell of a lot like pity.

Tristan thinks…who can he call? His mother? No way. His father? No fucking way. Cole? That's a lecture waiting to happen, same with Abby. He's got loads of contacts in his phone, but most of those are people who will carry him straight out of this bar and right into another one. He's done enough damage for one night, surely.

"Nah," Tristan says. "I'll call my driver."

The bartender nods and maybe rolls his eyes, probably writing Tristan off as just another rich asshole.

He's not wrong.

Tristan does call his driver, and it doesn't take long for Armando to pull up to the curb outside. When Tristan sees the shiny, familiar town car, he stumbles out of the bar, onto the sidewalk, and right into a person he didn't realize he wanted to see until he sees her.

CHAPTER
Five

*B*ecca's not sure why there are so many people on this particular block tonight, and she's trying not to get annoyed by all the jostling. You live in a city with millions of people whose primary mode of transportation is their feet, and there's bound to be lots and lots of jostling. She's just left her dinner with Abby, and she's cradling her precious box of homemade chocolates close to her chest, thinking happy thoughts about getting home and drawing a bath so she can sit and eat a few of these treats in luxurious peace.

She's doing a pretty good job of maintaining some zen in the chaos she's navigating, thinking her chocolatey thoughts, when a man basically walks right into her. He's a wall of muscle covered in a nice tailored suit and an expensive black wool peacoat. He smells like expensive cologne laced with whiskey. His hands linger on her upper arm and shoulder, and, if she's being honest, she has to admit that this is one of the nicest run-ins she's ever been part of.

"I'm so sorry," she says. The words just slip out, even though she's not entirely sure she's the one who walked into him. She's about to continue when she looks up and sees the man's tired, familiar face. Even after a long day that ended with copious amounts of drinking, Tristan Blackwell is still breathtakingly beautiful.

"Becca," he breathes. It's more of an inhale than anything, like he doesn't think she's actually real.

Becca's eyebrows draw together. Breathtaking beauty aside, he's clearly had a bad day. Becca supposes that's what he was trying to drink away. A wave of concern that she's not so sure he deserves washes over her, and even though she tries to fight it, worry manages to creep up on her.

"Tristan," she says, gripping his elbow and pulling them back toward the bar he just exited, out of the foot traffic. "Are you okay?"

He runs his fingers through his hair, obviously avoiding her gaze. He almost seems ashamed.

"No," he begins, looking at the ground. "I'm just…I'm not having a good day."

"Do you…" God, this is awkward. Becca shakes her head, trying to keep herself from stumbling over her words. "Do you need me to call someone for you?" She has to stop herself from asking him if he needs someone to help him get home.

Tristan pulls his phone out of his pocket and gives it a little wave. "No," he replies with a sad smile. "I can do it."

Becca bites her bottom lip, then says, "I know Cole's out of town, but Abby will pick up for sure. I don't know anyone else you know, obviously. Maybe you should eat? Do you need some food or something?" Becca really wishes she could just shut up already.

Tristan probably wishes she'd shut up too. He's rubbing the back of his neck, clearly uncomfortable. Maybe she should just go.

"I'm sorry," she says.

"For what?"

"I can't stop talking, and I'm making you uncomfortable."

"I like the babbling," he says, so softly that Becca almost doesn't catch it. "It's nice to know that you're concerned."

"Of course I'm concerned," Becca replies with a little laugh. "You're my best friend's husband's best friend." She lets out a sigh. "Wow, that's a mouthful."

Tristan laughs, and the sound of it delights Becca, even though it shouldn't. Thing is, he looks like hell and he's obviously had a terrible day, so the fact that she could make anyone smile in those circumstances makes her proud.

"Don't call Cole or Abby, okay?" he pleads. "Just…please don't do that."

"How are you going to get home?" Becca asks. "Can I get you a cab? Not that you take cabs, I mean…"

"I take cabs," Tristan says, with the hint of another smile as he points out at the street. "But tonight I called my driver."

Becca's eyes go wide. "A driver, of course. I don't know why I didn't think of that."

"It's good to see you, Becca," Tristan replies, completely

out of nowhere.

"Two days in four months. Must be some kind of record."

"Definitely a record." He lets his hand settle on her upper arm as he steps around her, headed for his car. "I'll see you?"

"Yeah, definitely." Becca's surprised to find that she means it. She's also surprised to see that Tristan looks lighter than he did when she first saw him, and she's a little reluctant to watch him walk away. Becca can't deny that she's curious about whatever it is that's going on with Tristan that has him not wanting her to call his best friend, and she doesn't feel comfortable leaving him alone when he seems to not be in a very good place. That's why she starts talking before she loses the nerve, before she thinks twice about what she's getting ready to offer.

"Tristan?"

He turns to her, his hand on the shiny black door of the waiting sedan. "Yeah?"

"Do you want some company? You seem kind of…I don't know. Seems like maybe tonight's not such a good night to be alone." She realizes about a second too late that she sounds an awful lot like she's offering sex, which she is most definitely not doing. "I mean, if you need a friend, I could be that friend."

He watches her for what seems like an eternity, then grins and holds out his arm, ushering her into the backseat of the town car. "A friend sounds pretty great right about now."

Becca and Tristan are standing in Tristan's apartment, and Becca can safely say that it's not at all what she was expecting. Not by a long shot.

It's a nice place, don't get her wrong, but truthfully, she thought he'd live in an apartment that was ridiculously over-the-top and ornate, like Abby and Cole's penthouse. She's not quite sure why she holds onto this ridiculous notion that all the wealthy people in New York live in apartments that have closets that would put her apartment to shame (although let's be real, most of them probably do), but this place doesn't even look like your typical mid-to-late-twenties bachelor pad. There's no sleek, utilitarian furniture. There's no modern art of questionable value, and the place isn't all black and chrome and completely devoid of any kind of color.

There are, however, the requisite floor-to-ceiling windows and beautiful view of the city skyline, so that's nice. Tristan's living room is on the small side and really cozy. There's a taupe sofa and love seat that manage to look modern *and* be fluffy enough to entice her into wanting to curl up onto them and relax into the pillows. Books with creases littering their spines are neatly stacked on his dark wood coffee table. Typical of a bachelor in his twenties, the focal point in the room is a large-screen television. The apartment has an open floor plan, and off to the side of the living room is a dining room that's not casual, and yet not fancy, either. It has an understated elegance to it, despite the fact that there's a bowl of what looks to be real fruit in the middle of it.

Tristan Blackwell lives in a small apartment and eats fruit out of a bowl that sits on the middle of his dining room table. She could laugh at all the ways he's surprised her just by letting her into his home.

Damn it, she's intrigued.

"Not what you were expecting?" he asks, looking like he needs to sleep for about a year as he slides off his jacket and slings it over the back of one of the dining room chairs.

"No," Becca replies, looking around. "And I mean that in the best possible way."

"I have another…" Tristan trails off, pursing his lips together like he's willing himself to shut up.

"Another what?"

"Nothing," he replies quickly. "It's not important."

Okay, so his mouth got away from him. Becca can't blame him for that, so she takes a deep breath and thinks of something to say that will help dissipate the air of awkwardness around them.

"Have you had anything to eat today?"

Tristan scrunches his eyebrows together, like he actually has to dig into the deep recesses of his mind to come up with an answer.

"No lunch? Nothing?"

He shrugs. "I was at my dad's office. I…I didn't really feel like eating."

Becca rolls her eyes and points toward the kitchen with her thumb. "How about I make you something to help soak up all that liquor?"

"You don't have to do that," he argues.

Becca pointedly ignores his protest and walks over to his pristine stainless steel refrigerator. "Do you even have anything in…whoa."

She vaguely registers the sound of a barstool sliding against the floor as she marvels at the fact that his fridge is fully stocked. There's catalog-quality neatness happening here, the fruits and vegetables are perfectly shaped, not the dented ones she always picks up at the bodega on the corner a block away from her apartment.

"I don't shop for that. Or cook any of it for myself, if that makes you feel any better."

Becca shoots him a playful glare over her shoulder. "You're telling me you don't have to shop and that you don't have to cook, and you expect that to make me feel better?"

Tristan lets out a soft laugh. "Yeah, maybe that wasn't the best thing to say."

Becca takes out some ground beef and digs around for some cheese before she sets both on the counter. She notices Tristan slumped against the counter of the island, cradling his head in his hands. Becca walks over to her purse and pulls out her pill case, dumps three ibuprofen in her hand, then walks over to the shelf next to the fridge where she saw glasses lined in a very neat row. She pulls one down and walks to the sink where she fills it with cool water.

"Here," she says, gently placing the glass and pills on the gray speckled granite in front of Tristan. "This will make you feel better."

Becca turns and starts opening and closing cabinets,

searching for a frying pan. Since Tristan admitted that he doesn't even cook, she figures it's pointless to ask him where they are. He'd probably say something ridiculous like, "What's a frying pan?" and she knows now is not a good time to laugh at the poor guy.

When she finally finds a pan, she places it on the burner and unwraps the ground beef. "I'm going to make you a cheeseburger, okay? Greasy comfort food is just what the doctor ordered. And that doctor is probably not a good one, because hello clogged arteries, but goodbye headache, I guess."

Tristan doesn't answer, and Becca turns and looks at him. He's staring down at the ibuprofen like they're a precious commodity, like they're water and he's dying for a drink.

"Those only work if you swallow them, you know."

She expects a sarcastic smile in return. What she gets is a look full of so much vulnerability that it almost takes her breath away.

"Why are you doing this?" he asks.

"Doing what? Giving you ibuprofen?"

"Being nice to me."

Oh, the crack in his voice just breaks her heart. Truth is, Becca's never really been one for holding grudges. "You seemed like you could really use a friend."

He swallows and nods, like words are too much for him right now.

"Why don't you go lie down on the sofa, and I'll come get you when this is ready?"

Tristan slides off the barstool and stands. "Sorry I'm not

much company right now."

Becca offers him a sympathetic smile. "Good thing I'm not here for company then."

"Good thing," he replies, and Becca thinks she might almost see a smile lurking on his lips.

"Go. Rest. I'll come get you when I'm finished."

CHAPTER
Six

*L*ying comfortably on his couch, Tristan lets his head sink into the soft pillow behind him as he closes his eyes and wills the ibuprofen to get to work on his aching head. Becca's tinkering in the kitchen becomes a distant din, and wow. The fact that she's even here is a development, but the fact that she's in his kitchen making him some kind of home-cooked hangover remedy? He's having difficulty wrapping his brain around that. When he ran into her at the benefit a few nights ago, he had some faint, distant hope that someday they might be friendly. Acquaintances at most.

Now look at them.

Running into Becca outside the bar was probably the luckiest Tristan had ever gotten while he was stumbling around, half drunk. She's like walking sunlight; just being around her brightens him up, even on a night like tonight when his head is pounding and he feels like shit. He's not sure why he would've expected differently, though. Of course being around her would be good for him; he's a mess and she's the furthest thing from one. What good does being around him do her?

His head is killing him, so he's not going to think about this anymore tonight. He's just going to enjoy her company and eat whatever it is that she's cooking in his kitchen that's making his apartment smell like heaven - he can't remember what she told him she was making.

He can remember that she told him to close his eyes and rest, so that's exactly what he does.

"Tristan?"

There's a warm hand on his shoulder, gently shaking him from side to side. It's almost like rocking, and it's definitely nice.

He cracks his left eye open and sees Becca sitting on the edge of his couch, right next to his thigh.

"Yeah?" he asks. He feels like he's been out forever, but not nearly long enough.

"You wanna eat?"

His stomach feels like a pit of burning fuel, hellbent on getting revenge. "Sure."

"C'mon." She offers him a hand as she stands, and then she helps him sit up.

Tristan takes a moment to get his bearings, gripping the edges of the couch to help quell his spinning head and reacquaint himself with gravity. "How long was I out?"

Becca shrugs. "Maybe fifteen minutes?"

Shortly after he shakes his head in disbelief, he realizes what an idiotic idea that is. "Really?"

Becca grins, probably at the disgruntled look on his face, and god. Even through the fog in his brain he can't help but think about how beautiful she is. A dangerous thought is what that is, and he needs to stop it right in its tracks.

"Really."

"I feel like I was out for hours." He feels like he was run over like a truck, but he doesn't tell her that.

"And you wanted to be out for more hours, right?"

"Right," he replies with a small laugh.

"Then let's get something in your stomach and then you can get to bed." She offers him her hand again, puts all of her weight into helping him up, and leads him into the kitchen. On the island, in front of the barstool he was sitting on earlier, is a greasy cheeseburger on a pristine white plate next to a glass full of something red.

Like she senses his curiosity, she says, "It'll help with a hangover. Try not to think about it too much while you're drinking it."

"What's in it?" he says as he lamely hops up on the stool. God, he's pathetic. How is she even still here with his sorry ass?

"You don't want to know. Although if it makes you feel any better, it's all stuff that I found in your refrigerator."

"That doesn't make me feel any better."

"That drink will make you feel better, if you *drink* it."

"This smells really good," Tristan says, pointedly ignoring the drink as he nods at the burger. It's greasy in an appealing way, and it's just what he needs after a night of a little too much drinking. He digs into the burger and *damn*, it *is* good. He must make some kind of hum of approval, because Becca's mouth lifts up into a smile.

"This is delicious," he says.

"It's a skill I picked up cooking for myself," she teases.

Tristan watches as she walks the dirty pan over to the sink and turns on the water. "You don't have to do that," he says. Then he shakes his head, because of course she doesn't *have* to. He doesn't *want* her to, is what it is. "Please leave that for me. I'll wash it in the morning."

She tosses her hair over her shoulder before she squirts dishwashing liquid onto a sponge. "It's either this or watching you eat. I think we're both better off if I just go ahead and do the dishes."

After Becca's finished washing the pan, she pulls out some kind of surface cleaner under the sink and starts spraying the counter to get rid of the grease splatter, Tristan guesses. She finishes wiping it off right as Tristan finishes his burger, and if he didn't feel badly for putting her out, he'd ask for another one. He stands, feeling better already, and walks over to the sink, where he deposits his dirty plate. When Becca makes a move to wash it, Tristan reaches out and puts his hand on her forearm.

Her skin is so warm and inviting. It's very soft, and he's

tempted to let his hand settle there and get lost in the memory of the way she felt against him that night they spent on the beach after Abby and Cole's wedding. They didn't talk about anything important, really, just stars and constellations. They teased each other relentlessly, and he was just Tristan and she was just Becca until Tristan couldn't think about anything other than the way his lips would feel against hers. So, he did what he always does and gave into his impulse and kissed her. Softly. Tenderly. He kissed her until he wanted more. It wasn't sex that he wanted necessarily, although he wanted that too, but he felt the strongest urge to talk to her more, to kiss her more. He wanted to thread his fingers through her hair and hold her close.

Probably sensing that he was a piece of shit who couldn't be trusted, Becca disentangled herself from him and headed for the house. Before she went inside, she asked him if she would see him at breakfast in the morning. Tristan knew that if he stayed for breakfast he'd never want to leave, and even though he wanted her so badly, he knew he wasn't equipped to give her the kind of relationship she deserved, and part of him wondered if some of his rich shine would wear off once she got to know him better, wondered if she was interested in him as a person rather than his checkbook. He wondered how badly it would hurt if he got attached and then found out there was more draw to his name and his money than there was to him.

It's happened to him before; it'll happen to him again. He's surrounded himself by so many hangers on these past few years that he's not sure he recognizes the good people from the bad.

So he told her yes, he'd be there in the morning, that he'd see her at breakfast. Then he went up to his room and got hard at the thought of her legs wrapped around his waist, the way he'd feel sliding inside of her. Restless and unable to sleep, he jacked off in the shower as he imagined her nipples, hard and pink, and what his name would sound like falling from her lips as she came.

He left shortly after.

He just packed his bag and hopped in the car, before the sun even came up, scared of what would happen if he stayed.

So, he followed his impulses again, only this time he ran away. Part of him knew he made the right decision, but part of him has regretted it ever since, and yet here she is, in his kitchen, being nice to him. He cannot even fathom why, but he knows that he's sorry for leaving her that day. He's sorry if he hurt her, and he's sorry that he's the kind of guy that she absolutely should not get mixed up with.

He's so fucked up. He's so worried about people wanting him for his money that he's afraid to get close to anyone, and he's got such a terrible track record with relationships that he doesn't want to hurt her even more than he already has. He's afraid to let her hurt him.

Things between them were doomed from the start.

"You okay?" she asks. From the look on her face, Tristan can tell he zoned out for a minute or two there.

"Yeah, I was just thinking."

"'Bout what?"

Tristan takes a deep breath and threads his fingers

together, and when he looks up at Becca, she's so…*open*. Her eyes are clear and she's obviously waiting, and something about it makes him feel comfortable telling her what he's really thinking. He has to get this out right just once, even though he's tried and failed several times before.

"I know you don't want to hear this again," he begins, chancing a look up at her. He sees her shift on her feet, can practically feel her muscles tense, even from where he stands on the other side of the island. "But…you're standing here being so nice to me when I really don't deserve it, and I wanted to tell you again just how sorry I am for taking off…for leading you on like I did." He swallows so hard that it *hurts*, because he hadn't led her on; he wanted what he initiated, but he wanted so much more than that and he knows, *he knows* he's a fuck up. He doesn't want to be a fuck up with her.

Becca is quiet for a few seconds, then leans forward, splaying her hands out on the granite between them. "Know what I think?"

Tristan shakes his head.

"I think that Cole and Abby have something special, and that when you're around them it's difficult not to get swept up in it. Going to weddings when you're single makes you start thinking about things, and there was a lot going around us that weekend. It's okay. Your best friend is married to my best friend. We've done a great job at avoiding each other the past few months, but…I don't want that. I don't want things to be uncomfortable for them, and I don't want things to be uncomfortable for us. I don't want us to see each other at a party and go in opposite directions. I don't want this... fracture."

"I don't want that either," Tristan says. He feels like shit about so many things in his life. So many things are wrong and unsettled, and he doesn't want to be unsettled in any part of his friendship with Cole and Abby. He doesn't want to be unsettled with Becca.

"So, why don't we forget that night ever happened and chalk it up to wedding feels," she says, smiling.

"Wedding feels?" he asks, laughing. He's surprised to realize that his head is feeling better already. He doesn't know if it's from the burger or the talk; maybe it's both.

"Yeah, it's a new term I'm using for when single people get all wrapped up in wedded bliss and do stupid things. We caught some wedding feels and they made us act stupid, but it's over now and we're adults, so..."

"Yeah, we're adults," Tristan repeats. He just cannot believe how this conversation is turning out.

"Okay, good. I'm glad that's settled," Becca says with a long exhale.

Tristan's glad too.

Becca reaches in her purse, pulls out her pill case, and puts three more ibuprofen on the counter. "I'm going to go, but here's a little safety net in case you wake up and your head's screaming."

Tristan smiles at her. "I'm feeling better already, but thank you. I don't know how I'm going to repay you."

Becca looks up at the ceiling and taps her chin, playfully pretending like she's thinking it out. Maybe she actually is thinking about it, he doesn't know. It's cute either way, and he knows that whatever she asks him for he'll give it to her.

"Well, I'm tempted to ask for a pony, but friends don't require repayment for being friendly, right?"

"Right," Tristan sighs, even though apart from Cole and Abby, that hasn't really been his experience. He's going to find a way to repay her anyway.

"One thing you can do for me is down that glass," she says, nodding at the hangover cure he still hadn't taken so much as a sip of. "I can only ignore the fact that you haven't drunk it yet for so long."

Tristan eyes it warily. He's sure he's had worse, even though this thing has a smell to it that's vaguely reminiscent of the kind of odor that would alert you to the fact that you have a broken garbage disposal.

Becca grabs another glass and fills it with water, then hands it to him and says, "You're going to want this when you're finished."

Tristan's going to want more than that when he's finished, he's sure. He steels himself and downs the drink, unprepared for how nasty it is, Jesus. Then he reaches for the glass of water and swallows almost all of it in one superhuman gulp.

"Good boy," she says, patting his arm before she takes the glasses and sets them in the sink. "Can I see your phone for a sec?"

Tongue burning, Tristan pulls his phone out of his pocket and hands it to her. She taps a few screens and types something before she places it back in his outstretched hand.

"How about next time you feel like drinking your face

off, you give me a call and we'll talk it out. No nasty hangover cure involved."

"But no delicious burger, either." He gives her a soft, playful pout.

"A burger could always be arranged," she teases. "If you ask. Deal?"

He nods, offering her a genuine smile. "Deal."

"Okay then," she sighs, sliding her arms through the sleeves of her jacket. "I'm going to head home."

"Please, let my driver take you."

Becca shakes her head. "No, I can get a cab. It's not too late, you know. Trains work too."

"I don't-"

"You don't have a say," she tells him. "If you loan me your driver, then I'm just going to pay him off to let me out at the nearest subway station, okay?"

He doesn't like that idea one bit, but still he says, "Okay."

"If you're worried about me getting home, you can always text me. You have my number now."

Something about the way she says that warms him up inside. "That I do."

"So, use it."

He's not even sure if she's flirting with him, or if this is just the way the two of them communicate: light and easy, like they've known each other forever.

Becca does let Tristan walk her out, as far as the subway station on the far corner of his block. When he's back at his apartment he takes a quick shower, and by the time he crawls into bed, he figures she must be home, so he shoots her a quick text.

Are you home?

He decides he's giving her five minutes to answer, and if she doesn't, he's going to make his way over to her place. Never mind the fact that he doesn't know where she lives; he'll worry about that later if he needs to. Also never mind the fact that this is the first time in his long, storied history with women that he's ever been so worried about whether or not one of them made it safely home, which gives him something to think about because it's a slap in the face confirmation that he really has been such a shit.

Tristan sits propped up against his headboard, his foot bouncing nervously under the sheet. He's fucked women who have had him less wound up than this. A burger and some post-drinking companionship, and he's already literally waiting by the phone. This does not bode well for Tristan, he knows.

Becca replies three minutes and thirty six seconds later.

I'm home. Get some rest.
Goodnight!

Tristan can't wipe the smile off his face.

Fuck, he thinks. *I'm in trouble.*

CHAPTER
Seven

The first thing Becca does when she receives the text from Tristan is enter him into her phone as a contact. Given the disappointment she felt when he disappeared the night after Cole and Abby's wedding, she knows this is probably a bad idea, but she does it anyway. Even though he was kind of hung over and having a terrible day, it was nice being around him. There's something about this man that just draws her in, she can't think of another way to explain it. It happened the first time they met and it's happening now. Thankfully her experience with him showed that it's probably for the best that they keep things on the platonic side (Becca really has no interest in getting into a situation she knows will likely end with a broken heart. *Her* broken heart.), she's just going to have to tamp down any other feelings of warmth and desire and hope that bubble up when she's around him.

She can do that. She totally can.

Like, right now when she's smiling at her phone, thinking of the soft way he apologized for hurting her and knowing that he really meant it. She rolls over and puts her phone on the nightstand.

Tamp, tamp, tamp.

She's restless, her mind racing as she thinks about work, about her grocery list, about Tristan. Ugh, she knew she was going to be in trouble if she let him into her life, but she figured she could fight it off for longer than an hour. How pathetic.

Whatever, she thinks it's nice to have things between them settled. Before, she'd get this rising, unstoppable feeling of anxiety whenever she thought Cole or Abby would bring up Tristan's name during dinner, worried that they were going to needle her or wondering how she'd talk them out of trying to set the two of them up again. Now things could be normal, and anxiety free. Tristan's name could be spoken freely and Becca wouldn't have to cringe every time she anticipated hearing it.

It's going to be good.

It's going to be *great*, as long as Cole and Abby mind their business and don't try to play matchmaker again. As long as Becca can keep herself from getting too attached, because he'll probably just wind up taking off again when she least expects it. Things will be going well, and…poof. Gone.

Her cell phone lighting up catches Becca's eye in the darkness.

I'm really glad I ran into you tonight, Becca.

Becca bites her lip to stop the smile and starts typing:

I'm glad I ran into you too. Best encounter I've ever had with a drunk guy outside of a bar, honestly.

He replies:

I wasn't drunk!

Followed by a quick:

Okay, I was half drunk.

Becca types:

You should be fully asleep by now. ;)

Becca yawns and stretches, and when she takes one last glance at her phone, she sees:

Ditto. Sleep well.

Becca snuggles into her pillow, thinking about him.

Tamp.
Tamp.

Tamp.

CHAPTER
Eight

*S*unday dinner is a tense affair in the Blackwell home. Clay and Tristan sit on opposite sides of the expansive, ridiculously ornate table. Charlotte, Clay's wife and Tristan's mother, tries making polite conversation throughout all six courses. It's a valiant attempt at breaking the tension between the two men she loves the most in this world, but it's a failure. The one topic of conversation that gets the most response from them is the news that she's been chosen to head the New Year's party committee at the country club the family has belonged to since before Tristan was born, and even that response was lukewarm.

Clay barely looks at Tristan throughout their meal, and when he does, it's an icy, angry, fleeting glance. Surely Charlotte knows that something is going on between them, although Tristan isn't sure that she knows exactly what it is. He wouldn't be surprised if his father told her about the fight they had in his office the other day, and he wouldn't be surprised if he didn't. What Tristan knows for sure is that his mother has a habit of sticking up for him, and if there's anyone who can tame the anger that wells up inside Clay Blackwell when it comes to his son, it's Charlotte.

After dinner is over, but before their cook brings out the dessert she made, Clay excuses himself from the table under the guise of having to attend to some business matters. Tristan knows he's probably just tired of being in the same room with him, where the tension is thick and the air between them is chilly. Tristan's willing to bet that he's not going to see his father again tonight.

After his father's hasty exit, Tristan notices that his mother is uncharacteristically quiet. He doesn't ask her about that right away; instead he picks at his custard for a while, until the curiosity is nearly killing him.

"Does he really have a call?" Tristan asks.

Charlotte sighs as she nearly drops her fork, and a loud clank rings out across the room. Tristan's struck by how tired his mother looks, and it makes his chest ache. She's still a relatively young woman, and she's all delicate bone structure and soft, pale skin, but the tension is taking a toll on her, he can tell.

"Tristan," she replies, wearily glancing over at him.

"I pissed him off the other day."

"Don't I know it." She rolls her eyes, and looks more frustrated with Tristan than she has in a while.

"You're on his side?" He's shocked and a little hurt,

honestly. He doesn't even try to hide it.

"I'm on the side that turns you into a responsible member of society, Tristan."

He practically glares at her, because Jesus. Her too?

"I am a responsible member of society, Mother. I pay my taxes. I have investments. It's not like I don't have a job, I just don't have the one that he wants me to."

"You own nightclubs, son. What kind of future is there in that?"

"A pretty damn good one, judging by my books."

"You know what I mean, Tristan."

"I do know what you mean," he replies, sitting back and throwing his napkin on the table next to his plate. He's not hungry anymore. "What you mean is that you'll only consider me a responsible member of society if I'm working at the company, being Dad's lapdog and claiming my birthright or whatever in the hell he likes to call it."

"No." Charlotte leans forward, resting her forearms on the edge of the table as she clasps her fingers together. "What I mean is that I don't want you ending up in those godawful gossip magazines that print pictures of you looking like you fell into a vat of liquor while parading a different model on your arm every week. What I mean is that I want you to settle down into a *life*, Tristan."

"You want me to get married."

"No, darling," she says, reaching for his hand. "I want you to find something that makes you happy. Can you honestly tell me that you're happy running around with models and getting drunk at benefits?"

Tristan looks down at his plate and fiddles with a berry. No, of course he can't look her in the eye and tell her that. It would be a lie, and he can't lie to his mother, no matter how ashamed he is of the truth.

As usual, she reads him like a book. "That's what I thought." She squeezes his hand and leans in closer. "I just want you to be happy."

"That's what *you* want. What dad wants is for me to be-"

"Dad wants you to take steps. He wants you to be…more. He wants you to be the kind of person he knows you *can* be."

He's twenty-eight years old. He shouldn't be having these conversations at this point in his life. Maybe he's not happy with his life right now, but he sure as shit isn't going to be happy with the life his father wants him to have either.

"Mom-"

"He wants you to take your place at the company, I can't deny that. He's wanted that since before you were born. He's talked about it since the moment he first felt you move in my belly. And that's not fair, I know it. It's a lot of pressure and expectation to put on a person. But if he saw you trying at life, really trying, then I think he'd wake up. He's always going to want these things for you, I won't lie. But if you made a little bit of effort…"

Tristan lets out a long sigh, but he doesn't say anything. There's nothing left to say. Trying only counts with Clay Blackwell if you're trying the things he wants you to. Everything else be damned.

On his way home from dinner, Tristan thinks about stopping off at a bar. He thinks about finding a party somewhere in the city, thinks about finding a friend that he knows he shouldn't be associating with. He wants to find a pretty girl he knows he shouldn't bring back to his bed, and he wants to lose himself in all the things he shouldn't be doing.

Thing is, all of the shouldn'ts don't hold any real appeal to him tonight. Tonight he wants something solid, something that isn't going to slip away in the morning.

When he's back at his apartment, he pulls his cell phone out of his pocket and scrolls down to the last text he sent Becca. He's been careful not to text her since that night; he doesn't want to push her too far or too fast, but she did tell him to text her if he ever felt like going to a bar, and he figures she's a woman of her word if ever there was one.

So, he types out a message:

Had dinner yet?

It's nearly eight, so he's not sure what kind of a response he's going to get. After a few minutes pass, Tristan wonders if she was actually serious about wanting him to text her. Maybe she's the kind of woman who doesn't respond right away, the kind of woman who wants to keep him on the edge of his seat and make him squirm when she can. Maybe she's sleeping, or maybe she's out with friends. Someone like Becca is sure to have a ton of them.

When he reaches peak doubt, the bubble pops up in the text window, letting him know that Becca's typing.

He tries and fails to ignore the wild swoop in his stomach as he waits for her response.

Had dinner and dessert! :)

Damn, he thinks. Then, he gets an idea.

Feel like watching a post-dessert movie?

A minute passes, then two.

Sure. Whatcha thinking?

He realizes that she must think he wants to meet her at a theater or something, and he's really not up for that.

I was thinking about something from my DVD collection. Your choice.

She replies a few seconds later.

Sure, I just have to change.

Without thinking, he writes:

Come in your pajamas. I'll send a car.

He expects her to argue, but surprisingly she doesn't.

Okay. Need my address?

He absolutely does.

CHAPTER
Nine

Sometimes, when Becca looks at her life, she can't help but realize that yeah, it's a little boring. Like when she's sitting on her couch on a Saturday night with an avocado skin clarifying treatment slathered all over her face, and she's clearing out her DVR instead of going out on dates and enjoying the city like other people her age.

Then there are the times when she can't help but realize that yeah, her life is pretty amazing. Like when she's wearing couture in the middle of a ballroom full of New York's elite, at a party for whatever occasion.

Then there are nights like tonight, when she can't help but realize that yeah, her life is unbelievable. Like when she walks down to the front door of her apartment building and finds a shiny black car waiting at the curb with a chauffeur holding the door open for her. When she's standing at

Tristan Blackwell's front door wearing pink pajamas with small white cartoon bunnies all over them.

She doesn't even know how she got here.

Well, of course she knows how she *got* here, got here. Tristan sent his driver over to pick her up after he texted her and asked her if she wanted dinner.

Becca and Tristan are becoming friends, building on this weird connection between them that makes her feel like she's known him for half of her life, even though it's pretty much been closer to three total days, if you add up all the time they've spent together so far. She told Tristan she wanted to be just friends because it's obvious to her that he wants to be just friends, but she knows that she's going to have difficulty ignoring that warm, rushing feeling that she gets when she's around him. She's definitely going to have a hard time ignoring the way she wants to put her lips on his, so she can see how close to reality her memory of kissing him is.

Becca knows all that is going to be so difficult for her, yet here she is anyway, knocking on Tristan's front door.

He opens it almost immediately, wearing a grey t-shirt and blue sweatpants. The t-shirt is…yeah, it's good. It clings to his muscled chest and abs, and Becca remembers what those abs felt like when she ran her fingers across the ridges of muscle that night on the beach. She never got a good look at him though, since Tristan was wearing a shirt that night and she stopped things before they got a little more naked.

Sometimes she wonders what she was thinking back then. Other times she thinks that stopping things was the best decision she's ever made.

Anyway, Becca's kind of gawking at Tristan. Are these his pajamas? She imagined him sleeping in something a little less…pajama-y. Like his underwear, or maybe nothing at all.

She shakes her head because she needs to stop thinking like that; nothing good can come of it, especially since Tristan made it clear that he was sorry for leading her on.

He's not interested in you as more than a friend, Becca, she thinks. *Keep it friendly Don't get too attached, you'll only get hurt.*

"Hi," Tristan says, grinning. He looks so happy to see her as he steps back and lets her inside.

"Hi."

"What's that?"

"Popcorn," Becca says, holding up the two plastic-wrapped bags in her hand.

"You told me you had dinner *and* dessert," Tristan replies. "This would be considered…"

"A movie night necessity. Since you're a billionaire and probably grew up on some kind of artisan popcorn from the hills of Bordeaux or whatever, I'm going to introduce you to the beauty that is microwave cheddar cheese popcorn."

Tristan laughs as he takes one of the bags from her, turning it over in his hands. "Cheddar cheese?"

Becca gives him an incredulous look. "Please tell me you're familiar with the magic of powdered cheese."

"Can't say that I am," Tristan replies, shaking his head.

Becca gasps in mock horror, pressing a hand to her chest.

"Are you telling me that you've never had instant macaroni and cheese? Powder, milk and butter?"

Tristan's nose scrunches up. "No, that sounds disgusting."

"Oh," she sighs, shaking her head. "I have so much to teach you about the real world, Mister 'I-have-a-cook-and-never-go-shopping.' No wonder your abs are so ridiculous." She makes a vague, sweeping gesture toward Tristan's middle, and before she has a chance to be embarrassed by her slip, Tristan moves the conversation right along.

"We're going to start with popcorn?"

Becca blinks. "What?"

A slow grin creeps across Tristan's handsome face. "You said you had a lot to teach me. Tonight we're going to start with popcorn?"

"Yeah," she agrees. "Popcorn. It's quick comfort food, and I figured since you texted me on a Sunday night for movie time, you must need some comfort. So." Becca pulls the bags out of their wrappers and opens Tristan's microwave. "We're going to pop this bag, and we're also going to use the little cheddar packet from this other bag, so it's like double cheese, which is amazing."

"So it's like cheese with popcorn instead of cheesy popcorn."

Becca nods proudly. "Now you're getting the idea."

"What do you we do with the bag we're stealing the cheese from?"

"We worry about that later," Becca says with a grin.

Thirty minutes later, they're sitting on the couch with orange fingertips and an empty bowl between them. There's an action movie playing on the big screen television. Becca let Tristan choose which one he wanted to watch, but he doesn't seem to be paying much attention. Random action noises play in the background: tension-filled score over squealing metal and throttling engines as two guys chase each other down a too-narrow street. Tristan's got his arm draped on the armrest, and he's drumming the edge of it repeatedly as he stares off into the distance, kind of in the direction of the television.

Becca considers herself a pretty intuitive person, so she knows Tristan's mind isn't here in this living room. Obviously, something's bothering him given that he invited her over at this hour. Becca gets the impression that Tristan doesn't have too many people in his life that he feels comfortable talking to, and if his clique is as full of hangers-on as it seems to be, she doesn't blame him. He has Cole, but for whatever reason, he doesn't seem to want to talk to Cole about what's bothering him, so she figures it's on her to lend him a sympathetic ear.

"Everything okay?" Becca asks as she wipes her fingertips on the paper towel that's all crumpled up in her lap.

Now she knows for sure that he's distracted, because he doesn't even realize that she's spoken.

"Tristan?" When he still doesn't answer, Becca touches his bicep, skin on skin, and he jumps a bit, eyes immediately meeting hers.

"What's the matter?" He looks panicked, like he thinks something might've happened while he wasn't paying attention.

"Nothing," Becca replies with a soft smile. "It's just that I can tell you're distracted, and I thought you might've invited me over because you needed someone to talk to about it. Not that you have to talk to me if you don't want to, I mean…"

"I like talking to you," he says. "That *is* why I invited you over. How could you tell?"

Becca shrugs. "Just had a feeling."

He nods, doesn't push it any further. "I usually go over for Sunday dinner at my parents' house. My dad and I are at an…impasse, I guess you could call it. Maybe the best way to explain it is to say that we're having an extended argument. I'm not really sure what to call it, but I do know that he's disappointed in me."

"What's he disappointed in you for?" Becca asks.

"He wants me to take over the family business."

Becca nods. She doesn't know much about what Tristan does for a living apart from the fact that he's invested in a couple of nightclubs in the city. She does know that the nightclubs are both profitable and popular, but that seems more like a hobby than a career. She's not sure that's something to base a life on, not that Tristan really needs the money. But the mind needs to be occupied, and club management doesn't seem like a whole lot of work for Tristan. Especially when you compare him to someone like Cole, who works almost non-stop. Not that she's comparing him to Cole; she's sure he's been compared to Cole enough to last a lifetime.

"You don't want to?"

"No," Tristan says sadly. "It's never been something that I wanted to do. Most of my life I've done what my dad wanted. Went to the schools he wanted me to go to, took the classes he wanted me to, got the grades he wanted me to, played the sports he wanted me to. I just…I can't do that anymore. Not with the rest of my life, you know?"

She nods, and suddenly, playboy, tabloid-splashing Tristan Blackwell makes so much more sense to her now. It's his way of getting out from under his father's thumb.

Before Becca can think of something to say, Tristan continues. "He doesn't like me."

"Tristan," Becca says, cutting him off. "That's not-"

"It's true," he replies, turning his sad eyes to her. "He has this idea of the kind of person I should be, and I don't think he'll ever like me until I become that person. Sometimes he tells me that Cole's the son he wishes he had." Tristan laughs, but Becca can see that it cuts him.

"Well." Becca lifts her legs up, folding them beneath her on the couch. "What kind of person does he want you to be? You're kind, you're thoughtful, and you're nice to be around," she tells him. "Those seem like important things to me."

"You're sugar coating, and you know it. You've seen me in magazines. My reputation precedes me."

"What's your point?"

Tristan gives her a severe look. "*That's* my point! I'm a fuck up, Becca. He thinks that getting me to take responsibility for the company will fundamentally change who I am."

"Is that who you really are? Or is that the person it's easy for you to be?"

Tristan fixes her with an intense stare that makes her wonder if she should've said anything at all.

"Sorry," Becca replies quickly. "I'm not trying to be a psychologist or anything. I know it can't be easy to have so much pressure on you, so it seems like the best way to deal with that would be to make people think that you can't handle responsibility."

Tristan takes a deep breath and sighs, then runs his fingers through his hair. "That's…that's surprisingly insightful."

Becca does her best to look offended. "You're telling me you're surprised I give good advice? I'll have you know that I am an excellent advice giver."

"I'm just surprised that you seemed to cut through my bullshit so quickly," he says with a soft laugh. "Have you always been the responsible one in your family?"

Becca shakes her head. "I don't have any brothers or sisters. My mom is an office manager for a supply company in Ohio, so I don't have quite the legacy to live up to that you do. All my mom ever wanted was for me to graduate from college and get a job in a field that I love; she never put any qualifiers on that. Seems like your dad has very specific ideas of what he wants for you, so I can see how that weighs you down and makes you want to rebel a bit."

"My mom told me tonight that all my father wants is for me to try. He doesn't think I'm responsible at all, and I guess he thinks making me his protege will instill some sense of responsibility into me."

"Well, you're not living on the street and your lights are still on, so I'd say you're at least a little bit responsible."

Tristan laughs. "Thanks."

"You know what I mean. I wasn't trying to insult you. I mean, you don't have responsibilities in the traditional sense, because you don't really need to work in order to make ends meet. So, all the things that someone would traditionally judge responsibility by are things you don't need to worry about."

Tristan nods, absorbing what Becca's telling him. "My mother's going in on me, too, only she's less concerned with me taking over the business and more concerned about me finally settling down."

"Is that not something you want?"

Tristan shrugs, then leans forward and rests his elbows on his knees. "It's not something I ever let myself think about, really. Clubbing, doing the shit I was doing…it's not a fulfilling life, but at this point I'm not really sure what is. And I…I don't really have the best track record at keeping good things going."

"So, maybe do this one step at a time. Find one thing that fulfills you and makes you happy, and maybe the rest will fall into place. Like puzzle pieces, or some other kind of cliche that I'm not thinking of right now."

"You make it sound easy," Tristan says.

"Probably because I've never had to do it," Becca replies with a smile. "It seems like you're making a good start though. You texted me tonight instead of going to a bar and drinking your face off."

"How did you know I wanted to go to a bar?"

"I'd probably want to go to a bar if I had dinner with your parents," she teases, playfully nudging him with her shoulder.

"You haven't had too many awkward family dinners, I take it?"

"No," Becca replies. "I'm lucky that way. But then again, I also don't have an obscene amount of money in my bank account, so it all evens out, I think. What do you say we pick a new movie that you can get invested in from the start? Turn your brain off for a little while?"

"That sounds good," he replies, relaxing back into the sofa. "Why don't you pick this one?"

"You've got yourself a deal." Becca stands and walks over to the wall of DVDs. It seems like he has more movies here than there are books in an actual library. It's a little bit ridiculous, honestly.

"Becca?"

"Yeah?" Becca turns around and sees Tristan looking at her intently.

"I didn't invite you over here to distract myself from something else I'd rather be doing."

"Okay," she replies, not sure where this is going.

"I like being with you. That's why I asked you to come over."

Becca's traitorous heart speeds up, and she tries to push back the rush that accompanies the words he just said. He's not interested, *he's not interested,* don't get your hopes up, Becca.

"Yeah?" she asks. She just can't help herself.

"Yeah." He's giving her this look that makes her want to crawl onto his lap and kiss his troubles away.

Instead, she turns and picks a DVD. She has a feeling that she'll be the one distracted during this movie.

CHAPTER
Ten

The Sunday night that Tristan spends watching movies with Becca is the one that changes everything. That night makes the tentativeness between them just melt away, and Tristan can't get enough of her. Instead of finding oblivion at the bottom of a bottle in one hot spot or another, he finds whatever happiness he can with her.

They text each other almost constantly, and they call each other often. Sometimes he shows up with dinner at her doorstep when he knows she's had a long day, and he'll stay after their plates are empty to fix a broken closet door or walk with her to the bookstore at the corner of her block so she can buy the latest bestseller she's desperate to read. Day by day Tristan starts feeling some of the broken pieces inside of him shifting back together again, and it's all because of Becca.

Thing is, he's getting in too deep. He knows this, can feel it every time his heart starts beating faster when he sees her, or the way he can't help but smile when his phone lights up with a text from her. All this time they're spending together is so great, but it's getting more and more difficult not to kiss her. She smiles at him all the time (smiling seems to be a constant state for both of them when they're around each other), and he just wants to put his mouth on hers and taste the sweetness of her tongue. He remembers the way she felt when she melted against him that night on the beach; it haunts him sometimes, especially now that she's almost constantly within reach, and he's starting to forget why he thought being in a relationship was a bad idea.

When he watches her eat, her delicate fingers curled around the handle of a fork, he remembers what they felt like sliding through his hair when he kissed her for the first time over the summer. He remembers the way her breasts felt against his chest, and he wants to feel that softness again. He wants to slide his hands up her sides, slip her shirt off and taste her skin. He wants to suck that spot on her collarbone that's constantly peeking out from behind the collar of her blouse, and mark her as his.

He just…*wants* her all the time. It's a Herculean effort to keep his hands to himself, and one day he knows he's going to slip up. He's going to slip up, and he doesn't even want to think about what the fallout from that will be.

What makes it all worse is that he knows she wants him, too, although he can't imagine why. Within hours of meeting her he proved to her that he can't be trusted with her heart.

So the wanting on her end must be purely physical, but for him it's so much more. He's determined to hold out, to defeat it, especially now that he knows what he has with her. He doesn't want to do anything to ruin that.

When Becca gave Tristan her phone number, he was certain that he was the only one who was going to benefit from their friendship, and so far he has. He's called her over after a disastrous talk or dinner with his parents, but she actually calls him too. She's started looking for the same support from him, which shocks the hell out of him. He never anticipated that he would be as good a friend to her as she is to him, but god, he's trying. It's the one thing in his life that he doesn't want to fail at.

That's why he's standing in his apartment, waiting for her to arrive. She just called him, fresh out of a long day of meetings. She'd been taken to task by her boss because of a mistake she'd made in one of her accounting audits. She's still new in the position, having been promoted over the summer, and she's not taking the mistake very well.

Tristan gave her the address of a place where he wanted her to meet him. He considered going to pick her up, but she's just around the corner, and he needed to run across the street to pick up a bottle of Becca's favorite wine.

When the doorman calls Tristan to let him know that Becca's arrived, he swallows down the nervous swoop that makes its way up from his stomach. He knows he needs to get himself in check because this is how he usually feels before a date, and this is most definitely not a date. None of their meet-ups have been dates, and he can't start thinking of them like they are because once he goes down that road, it'll get harder and harder to find his way back.

Becca knocks on the door, and when Tristan opens it he can see how utterly exhausted she is. He wants nothing more than to slide his hand along the column of her neck and pull her close to him. Somehow, he manages to not do that.

"Hey," he says, reaching forward and taking her messenger back from her as she walks through the door. Her eyes light up when she sees him, and Tristan does his damnedest not to read too much into that. "You okay?"

Becca nods, even though Tristan can clearly see that she's not okay. He gives in to his earlier impulse and wraps his arms around her, holding her tight. She buries her face in his neck like it belongs there, and she breathes deep. With just that simple action, she relaxes into him. Her muscles lose a lot of their tension.

"Tell me what happened," he says, still holding her.

"I'm just stressed out," she replies with a sigh. "I have so much work to do, and budget cuts mean that I don't have as much help as I need. I got tired after a long day and I shouldn't have been working. I should've shut down and gone home, but my work was piling up and I didn't want to leave it, so I made a mistake. I cost the company, well…a lot of money. I hate messing up like that, and I worked *so* hard to get where I am. I'll be devastated if I get fired."

Tristan runs his fingers through her hair as he rocks her from side to side. "You're not going to get fired," he tells her, even though he has no way of guaranteeing that. He even considers making a joke about how he'll buy her company and rehire her if they even dare fire her, but instinctually he knows that kind of show of wealth isn't what she needs right now. Instead, he just keeps his mouth shut and his ears open as she tells him about her terrible day. When she looks up at him and disengages from his body, she steps back and wipes her eyes. Tristan thinks it's probably a good idea to get her some tissues, so he walks into the bathroom and grabs the box. When he returns, Becca's standing in the middle of the living room looking around like she's in some kind of museum.

"What is this place?" she asks as she pulls a tissue from the box and then dabs at her eyes.

Tristan grins. "I told you I had another place."

When Becca gives him a watery laugh, Tristan can't help but think about how pretty the sound is. "I thought you were kidding."

"I never kid about real estate."

Becca walks over to the large fireplace at the far end of the room and runs her fingertip along the mantel as she looks at the pictures sitting on top of it. "You don't live here…why, exactly?"

"It's too big of a place for just me," Tristan admits. "My apartment is better suited for the single life."

"So this is where you bring all the ladies?"

Tristan's heart sinks when he hears her poking fun at his checkered romantic past. He knows she doesn't mean it, but it's a sore spot for him all the same. "Not all the ladies," he tells her quietly. "Just you." He briefly wonders what he's doing, telling her things like that. "I come here often though."

"But you don't live here. It's bigger and nicer, and-"

"Empty?"

"Apart from the high-end furniture and decorations. Yeah." Her eyes go wide when she realizes what she's implying. "I mean, your place is nice too. I like your place a lot. I just wasn't expecting this." The blush creeps up her cheeks, and Tristan enjoys the look on her.

"You haven't seen the nicest part of it," he tells her, holding out his hand. She takes it without hesitation. "I come here sometimes when things in my life get to be a little bit too much. C'mon." He leads her across the room. "Let me show you why."

When they step out on the stone balcony that stretches the length of the apartment, Tristan smiles at Becca's loud gasp. At first he thinks it must be because of the crisp night air (which is warm for a November evening, but still not *warm*), but when he sees her face, he knows she's in awe.

"Wow," she whispers, the twinkling lights of the city's skyline shining in her eyes.

"You like it?"

Becca nods slowly. "I love it."

"Makes your problems seem kind of small, doesn't it?" Tristan lifts his arm for Becca to slide under, and she does that quickly, tucking herself against his side.

"It really does," she replies, wrapping her arms around his waist.

It feel so right, standing here with her like this. Tristan's not sure he'll ever have this chance again, so he decides he's going to enjoy it while it lasts.

There are an obscene number of empty Chinese food containers scattered on the table, and they've had nearly a bottle of wine between them. It's late, and they should definitely go home, but Tristan just doesn't want to leave. He doesn't want to stop talking to her. He's feeling the beginning of a very mellow, pleasant buzz from the wine, and the company couldn't be better.

"Tell me about how you grew up," Tristan says as he reaches for his wine glass.

"What do you want to know?" There's a beautiful flush in Becca's cheeks, and Tristan wants to feel the warmth of it with the palms of his hands.

"Everything," he replies honestly.

Becca laughs. "I grew up in Ohio, there's absolutely nothing interesting to tell."

"That can't be true," Tristan says, shaking his head. He can't imagine anything about her being boring.

Becca pauses, and for a second he wonders if there's some deep, dark past that she's hiding and afraid to tell him about. It's ridiculous, of course, but she's clearly hesitant to share that part of her life with him. Just when he's about to tell her that she doesn't have to tell him anything that she doesn't want to, she starts speaking.

"I grew up in a really small apartment with my mom. My parents got divorced when I was really young; I don't really remember much about my father. I saw him sometimes, but he didn't show up very regularly, and he certainly didn't pay child support very regularly, so…times were tough for us. My mom made do, though, but I never realized how bad things were until I was older and began to understand just how much some things cost and how far my mom had to stretch every dollar she earned. Somehow she always managed to make sure that I was able to do things the other kids did. If I wanted to play soccer, I had a clean uniform and cleats and my registration fees were paid on time. If I wanted to go on a field trip, she'd eat ramen for dinner for weeks." Becca pauses and swallows, and even in the dim light of the dining room, Tristan can see she's holding back tears.

The thing about it that absolutely fascinates Tristan is that these aren't sad tears. Becca's got this far-off look in her eyes, like she's remembering one of the most beautiful times in her life. Tristan's desperate to reach across the divide between them and kiss her.

"She'd make penny pinching into some kind of game for me, like, she'd challenge me to contests to see who could fill up their side of the grocery cart with the most healthy stuff for the least amount of money. I thought it was fun at the time, but I realize now that she must've gone to bed really hungry some nights. She just made everything so fun that I didn't even realize anything was off, like when we couldn't afford to buy a Christmas tree and we decorated a wall in our apartment with ornaments we made out of construction paper and glitter."

Now Tristan knows how Becca became such a remarkable woman.

"My mom, she's a great person. She gave me a really great life, and when Abby's mom died, she took her in too. She always told me that she wanted me to be better than she was, to do better than she did, but I always wanted to be just like her."

Tristan reaches over and wraps his fingers around hers, thankful when she doesn't pull away.

"You are," he says quietly.

"What do you mean?"

"You said your mom had a way of distracting you from how bad things were," Tristan tells her, running the pad of his thumb over the backs of her knuckles. Her skin is so soft.

"Yeah…" Becca seems unsure of where he's going with this.

Tristan just can't believe that she doesn't understand what he's trying to tell her, so he's going to be clearer about it this time. He reaches up and cups her face, just like he's wanted to do for weeks now, and then he leans forward until his forehead is touching hers. He doesn't worry about what she might want from him, he doesn't worry about screwing this up. He just tells her the truth.

"Becca," he whispers. "You do that for me."

CHAPTER
Eleven

*B*ecca's not sure if it's the wine, the compliment Tristan just gave her, the undeniable sexual tension that's been building up between them since the day they met, or the fact that his lips are *this close* to hers. He's cradling her face in his hands and his lips are so close, and why did she ever think that being with him like this was a bad idea?

Oh, right. Her heart. She didn't want to get her heart broken, because one day she just knows she's going to go looking for him and he'll be gone again, but tonight she doesn't care.

It's pounding beneath her ribcage and she can't help but think about how strong it feels. It could withstand whatever cracks Tristan puts in it, she's sure. She had convinced herself that he wasn't interested, but he looks pretty interested right now as he holds her close, gazing at her, his eyes all soft and wanting. Then he just has to go and lick his perfect lips, *ugh*.

Becca's sure she's not imagining the way Tristan moves closer, the way his thumbs glide along her cheekbones. Nope, not imagining that at all.

She wants this, she's tired of fighting it. She's going to reach out and take it.

Becca reaches up and clasps her fingers around Tristan's wrists, needing something to hold onto.

"Becca," Tristan whispers, his voice absolutely wrecked. "I'm going to kiss you now."

Yep, those are the best words Becca's heard in a long, long time. Kissing's good, she wants the kissing. Of course, it's not the first time they've kissed; they did plenty of that the night of Abby and Cole's wedding. This time, though, it means something. Becca knows this, she can feel it all the way down to her bones.

Becca licks her lips as Tristan moves in and when he finally kisses her, it's warm and wonderful. He tastes just like she remembers, and he's kissing her like he's drowning and she's the only way he can breathe. She lets her fingertips slide up through his hair and around the back of his head so she can hold him close, just where she wants him, and she loses herself in his kiss. She loses herself in *him*, the feel of his mouth and the way his stubble scratches her sensitive skin as his mouth moves unrelentingly against hers, slow and soft and perfect.

She could die like this and be happy, she thinks, with his body moulded against hers and the taste of his tongue on her lips.

Actually, she'd be happier if she was sitting on his lap. Yeah, yep, on his lap seems like the place to be.

Reluctantly, Becca pulls away, and she can't help but smile at Tristan's disappointed groan. When she stands up, Tristan looks confused for a second before she motions for him to close his legs. He's so make-out rumpled and cute, she can't help but smile at his disheveled hair and half-lidded eyes. In fact, he looks so dazed she's not even sure that he knows what she's asking him to do.

"What?" he asks.

"Close your legs and turn a little," she tells him.

His eyebrows scrunch together.

"I want to straddle you," she says, and she sees the exact moment when he registers what she's saying.

"Jesus," he sighs, turning his chair a little for easy access, then he slides down a little for even easier access. "Yeah, straddling, thats…that's good."

Tristan gently lays his hands on Becca's hips as she walks forward, towering over him for a brief moment before she sits down. Tristan sucks in a deep breath, because Becca knows she's touching him *just* right; she can feel his erection between her legs, and she wiggles a bit just to torture him.

Tristan responds by pulling her down and crashing his lips against hers, and this time it's much more heated and desperate. Becca wants nothing more than to feel his warm skin, so she grabs the hem of the navy blue henley he's wearing and pulls up. Tristan moves to accommodate the lifting of his shirt, breaking the kiss to get his head through the neck hole, which gives Becca just enough time to admire the view.

God, seeing him is worth the wait.

His body is beautiful. He's got a broad chest and rippling muscles that are solid but not obnoxiously big. She likes watching the way his biceps move as he slides his hands up and down the outsides of her thighs. She reaches out and presses her palm against the center of his chest, feels the rapid thumping below it, and notices the goosebumps that seem to bloom on every inch that her hand touches.

Tristan starts unbuttoning her blouse, but the buttons are tiny and his hands are clumsy and huge, so when he gets impatient with the whole process, he reaches up and wraps his fingers around the placket and just rips it off. Becca's eyes are wide with surprise, and she can't hold back the little huff of laughter that escapes her lips. She's quieted, though, when she sees the look on Tristan's face when he leans back to get a good look at her. They're both breathless and panting, and he's looking at her like he wants to *devour* her.

She's going to let him.

Tristan's hands slide up her sides, coming to rest beneath the swell of her breasts. His thumbs glide along the edges of the lacy cup of her bra, and then slide back and forth over the fabric that covers her nipples. He's teasing her, and she likes it.

Becca wants Tristan so badly, she's actually aching for him. She wants his mouth on her, and like he can read her mind, he peppers her jaw with soft, tender kisses, trailing all the way down the column of her neck to her shoulders. When he reaches her bra strap, he slides it down, then makes his way to her other shoulder where he repeats the action.

"You're so beautiful," Tristan says against her skin, like he wants to make the words a part of her body. He unclasps her bra and tosses it aside once Becca slides it down her arms. Tristan doesn't wait a second before he's laving his tongue along the swell of her breast, then licks and teases her nipple between his teeth. His stubble is rough and scratchy against the tender skin, and she pushes into it; she wants more, she wants to feel the pleasant ache of it after this is over.

Becca leans forward and kisses Tristan's earlobe, then slides her lips along the length of his jawline, nipping at him in a way that he really likes if the shiver that runs through his body is any indication. It spurs her on, makes her want to see what else she can make him respond to. So, she rocks her hips against him, grinds against his erection. His head falls back against the chair and he pushes up, wanting and needing more friction.

"Becca," he says lowly, his voice nearly a growl. "If you don't stop that, I'm gonna come."

Becca absolutely does *not* stop that. In fact, she does it again, then licks a stripe along the side of his neck and gives it a gentle blow. "Isn't that the point?"

"I want-"

He's interrupted when Becca shifts her hips again, stopping right in the middle of his sentence. She's relentless, rocking against him.

"I want to be inside you when I do."

Becca grins wickedly, leaning back as she tucks her hair behind her ear. "Then get inside me."

Tristan's breath catches, and it's like everything slows down at once.

"Hey," Tristan breathes, cradling Becca's head in his hands.

This is beginning to be her favorite feeling—the callouses on his palms against the apples of her cheeks—because it's always accompanied by the soft but intense look in his eyes, like he can see every little thing she's thinking.

"Yeah?" Becca reaches up and swipes at her lipstick that's all smudged along his bottom lip.

"I don't know what you're thinking, but this is…" Tristan looks down for a moment, almost like he's ashamed. "I know I have a reputation, but this, this isn't like that."

Becca's not really sure what he's getting at here. "Not exactly like what?"

Tristan leans forward and gives her a tender kiss. "This isn't me fucking you at a dining room table like…like it's nothing, okay?"

Becca lips stretch into a slow smile. "I know it isn't." She slides her fingertips along the curve of his chin, struck by a sudden wave of tenderness, cresting beneath her chest. She stands and unzips her skirt, letting it fall to the floor, all the while thankful that she picked a matching bra and panties to wear today.

Tristan reaches out and runs the backs of his fingers along the sides of Becca's hips, and then his palms slide back around the curve of her ass. Her breath hitches and her head falls back, eyes closing as she enjoys the sensation. Soon she begins to miss the feel of him between her thighs, so she reaches down and undoes his pants, then grips the waistband and pulls, dragging his underwear along with his jeans. Tristan lifts his hips to help her, but before she can toss his pants aside, he reaches in the back pocket and removes his wallet, sliding a condom out of one of the slots.

Becca's thankful he's prepared. She unwraps the condom and rolls it down his long, thick cock, which is rock hard for her. She runs her fingertips down the insides of his thighs, delighting in the different ways she's learning to make his body react to her. He's just staring at her with half-lidded eyes, still managing to look like she hung the moon, and she can't wait another second for him to be inside of her.

Becca starts to kick her shoes off, but Tristan puts his hand on her hips.

"Leave the heels," Tristan says, voice absolutely wrecked.

Happy to oblige him, Becca stands so that she's straddling him again. Just when she's about to lower herself onto him, his hand moves between her legs and he slides his fingertip along the wet, wanting part of her, gently flicking her clit. Teasing. He kisses and licks his way across her belly, until finally Becca just can't take it anymore and she threads her fingers through his hair.

Tristan closes his eyes and lets out a deep breath; Becca can feel it against her belly.

"Need you," Tristan grits out, his voice low and rough.

Becca doesn't need to be told twice, and she's close to the brink herself, so she lowers herself down, bringing the tip of his cock to her entrance.

Tristan grips Becca's hips, and then gently, slowly, she

sinks down onto him as he lets out a long, ragged breath.

"Fuck," he whispers, dropping his head to rest on the delicate curve of her shoulder.

Becca rocks her hips back and forth, and Tristan slides his tongue around her nipple before he takes it into his mouth. The feeling of his mouth on her skin as he slides in and out of her is almost too much, and Becca grips the hair at the nape of his neck to ground herself as she rides him, feeling so full. He's hitting her in just the right spot; she feels the electric pleasure shooting all the way down to the soles of her feet.

"You feel so good," Becca manages, her lips pressed against the shell of Tristan's ear. "*So* good."

"Yeah?" He punctuates the question with a forceful thrust that makes Becca cry out.

"Mmmm-hmmm."

Tristan drags his lips along her collarbone, his raspy stubble scratching her skin. She wants to feel like this forever, wants to remember every single sensation every minute for the rest of her life. She tilts her head back, leaving her neck on offer for Tristan's kisses as he pushes her higher and higher and *higher*.

Just when Becca feels her orgasm building, Tristan picks her up. One arm is holding her securely against his chest, the other is cradling her head. He sets her down carefully, tenderly. Tristan barely gives her a moment to get her bearings before he lifts her left leg and slings it over his shoulder. Oh, this is the perfect height. This is the perfect *angle*. Becca wants to write a poem about how perfect this table is and how perfect Tristan is making her feel while he's fucking her on top of it.

It's perfect, did she mention that? Completely per-

Oh, god. He's hitting her g-spot with every single thrust; she can feel herself coming apart at the seams. So of course Tristan leans down and kisses her. He kisses all the breath out of her, leaves her panting and wanting more. Then he pulls away and licks the pad of his thumb and rubs her clit. Clockwise, then counter, winding her right up until she's about to spin right out of her skin.

When Becca comes, her back arches as pleasure radiates in waves throughout her body. She feels like her skin is on fire, and she can't get hot enough. Looping her arm around the back of Tristan's neck, she pulls him down for a slow, languid kiss. The movement is just enough to set her off, and she's coming hard and fast in waves that leave her boneless and breathless. When she finally comes down, she can tell that her orgasm felt almost as good to Tristan as it did to her, judging by the way his muscles tighten and his eyes shut tight as he tries to fight off his own pleasure.

Wanting Tristan to feel as good as she does, she lowers her leg and slides down to the very edge of the table, opening her legs as wide as she can before she wraps her hands around the sides of Tristan's waist and pulls him closer, wanting him deep, *deep* inside her.

Tristan plants his hands on either side of Becca's head and picks up the pace, pumping into her relentlessly. Becca kisses up the side of his neck and when she reaches his ear, she tugs the lobe between her teeth, then gently licks away the sting.

"Come on," she says, scraping her nails across his shoulders. He's trembling, teetering on the edge of his control, and when a second orgasm sneaks up and hits Becca hard, Tristan follows her into it. His thrusts grow frantic and unsteady as he sucks at her neck, his fingers twining through hers and squeezing as he comes inside of her.

They hold each other as they both come down, peppering soft kisses across sweat-glistened skin. Once she's finally breathing normally, Tristan lifts Becca and carries her into the bedroom. His bed is plush, and Becca can't hide her mewl as she sinks down into the cloud-like mattress.

Tristan crawls in beside her and turns her on her side, pulling her back against his chest until they're spooning.

"You have no idea how long I've wanted to do that," he says, his scruff rubbing against her temple before he drops a kiss there.

"Since the gala?" Becca twines her fingers with Tristan's as he wraps his arm around her belly.

He laughs, a quick huff that cools the beading sweat on the back of her neck. "Before," he says before he sucks on the skin there. "Way before."

Becca knows that he's talking about that night at the beach house, but they've agreed to leave that mistake behind them, so she doesn't ask him to elaborate. Instead, she snuggles against him and brings his hand to her mouth, planting a soft kiss on the back of it, right below his knuckles.

"I'm glad we got our chance then," she says.

Tristan slides his other hand up along the outside of her

thigh, around her hip, across to her belly button, and then lower. *Lower.*

"I think I'm ready for a second chance," he whispers.

Tristan's growing erection is straining against her ass, and all she can think about is letting him have all the chances he needs.

CHAPTER
Twelve

Tristan wakes before Becca, much earlier than he usually does. Early morning light is barely streaming through the windows; the sun is just beginning to rise. He's content in a way that he hasn't been in a long time, all relaxed and rested with a soft, warm Becca in his arms. He thinks about waking her, thinks about kissing her until her eyes open. He thinks about rolling Becca over until she's on her back, sliding his hands down the insides of her knees until she opens up for him. He wants to taste her, wants to lick her soft, wet skin until she writhes against his tongue, her fingers pulling his hair in the way he likes so much. What he really wants is to be inside her again, but he knows he needs to give her body a breather.

He sucked his way across a good amount of her surface area last night, leaving marks she'd remember long after they said goodbye. That thought makes his chest lurch. He doesn't want to say goodbye to her, and he allows himself to feel the jagged edge of annoyance about it. He knew once he finally stopped holding back from her that he'd be insatiable, that he'd want every part of her he could have, every waking moment he could have her.

Becca looks so peaceful here in his bed. She looks *right* here, like she's the piece of Tristan's life that he didn't know he was missing.

He shakes his head, trying to rid himself of that thought. It's too soon to be thinking things like that, and it's probably just the afterglow making him feel things stronger and faster than he normally would. Still, there's no denying that she's special to him, becoming more so by the day, and even though he can't really tell her how he's feeling, he can definitely show her.

Becca's lying on her side, her soft, full breasts pressed against his chest. She's using his bicep as a pillow. Her mouth is slightly open, and she's not really snoring, but he can hear her breathing. He likes the steadiness of it, likes the rhythm that it brings into his life.

Tristan slides his fingers through Becca's hair, pushing it back behind her ear, and she starts to rouse from her sleep. Her eyelids squeeze shut and her brows knit together as she mumbles sleepy, angry protests. Early morning Becca is cuter than she has any right to be, and Tristan continues his course of action, steadily trying to wake her up. Last night she told him that she was catching an early flight to Ohio to spend Thanksgiving with her mother.

Tristan wants to take her to the airport, and he knows they only have a little bit of time before they need to leave. He wants to make the most of it and send her off with a smile. He wants her to be thinking of him every second that she's away.

When Becca's eyelids flutter open, she gives him a surprised smile. It hurts Tristan to think that part of that surprise is because he's still there, that he didn't run from her in the middle of the night. He knows he has a long way to go to earn her trust, and he's going to do any and everything it takes to do just that.

"Morning," Tristan says.

Becca stretches out like a cat in the sun and lets out this adorable little mewl as she presses her breasts against him.

"Morning," she replies sleepily. She turns her head and kisses the inside of his arm.

Tristan never thought such a simple gesture would turn him on, but he's already half hard, and he can't resist bending forward and sucking on Becca's left breast. She sighs and runs her fingers through his hair, cradling the back of his head and pressing him against her.

"This is a *really* nice way to wake up," Becca says, her voice all light and airy, and Tristan agrees.

It's been forever since Tristan's wanted to spend the day in bed with someone, but he wants to spend it here with her. Not even having sex (although that would be nice), he just wants to *be* with her, to hold her, to learn everything there is to know about her while he holds her in his arms.

"What time is your flight?" he asks.

"Three hours." She sounds almost a disappointed as he feels. "I should probably go. I still have to pack some stuff, and then I need to get to the airport."

An idea hits Tristan. It's the kind of thing he used to offer to impress some of the girls he fucked, so it feels a little wrong offering it to her, but he just wants her to *stay*. Even a few extra minutes would be worth it.

"Please stay," he says, surprised by the fact that he almost sounds like he's begging. Maybe he would if he thought it would change her mind.

"I can't," she says, her voice catching as Tristan kisses his way across her chest. "If I miss my flight and don't show up, my mom will be so disappointed."

Tristan looks up at her. "I'll call and get the jet ready. If you fly that way, then you won't have to leave so early. We'll still have an hour or…"

Becca rolls her eyes. "You are *not* lending me your jet."

Tristan finds some comfort in her denial, realizing that she's the first person he's ever offered it to that's turned it down. That makes him want her to use it all the more.

"Why not? That's what it's there for, and I'm driving to the house in Connecticut to spend Thanksgiving with my parents, so I don't need it."

"Do you have any idea how absolutely ridiculous that last sentence sounded?" she says, laughing.

"I want you to take it. I'm serious."

Becca looks at him, giving him this soft, almost sad smile as she caresses his cheek. "You don't have to do that, you know. That's not why I'm here."

Tristan nearly laughs, because the last thing anyone would ever accuse Becca Smith of is being a gold digger. Although, if he's honest with himself, he's not really sure why she's here. He's a fuck up, he doesn't have anything going for him, he's going to break her-

"Hey," Becca says softly, pulling him out of his thoughts.

"I know that's not why you're here," he tells her before pressing his lips to hers. "That's why I'm offering it."

Becca rolls over onto her back, letting her arm fall across her forehead as she stares up at the ceiling. Tristan feels hope welling up inside him, because for a few seconds he thinks she might actually be trying to talk herself into accepting his offer. Hoping to persuade her, Tristan braces himself on his arm, holding himself over her as he kisses her deeply. She melts against him for one glorious moment, but before Tristan can fall too far, she's pushing at his chest.

"I want to," she says, absentmindedly tracing a pattern across his chest. "I want to stay with you, but I can't let you start offering me things like use of your *plane,* Tristan."

"Okay," he says, trying hard to hide his disappointment. Even though he genuinely wanted her to take it, he falls for her a little more when she doesn't.

Thanksgiving in the Blackwell household isn't a normal holiday affair like it is for most people. There is no extended family, there is no warmth in their togetherness. There's a gourmet meal that anyone would be lucky to have, eaten by three people sitting as far away from each other as possible. Halfway through the meal Tristan's father excuses himself for work, and his mother starts talking about what she's planning for the New Year's party she's holding at the club they belong to. Tristan does his best to pay attention, but he can't help but let his mind drift, thinking of Becca and hoping she's having a better holiday than he his.

He's surprised by how much he *misses* her, and she's only been gone for a day.

It's that realization that pushes him headlong into another one: he's in deeper with Becca than he ever imagined he could be. It's kind of shocking to him just how much the thought doesn't scare him. He likes being with her, and he can't stop thinking about her. He's just going to enjoy it while it lasts, not look too much into it to the point where he freaks himself out and ruins what is turning out to be one of the best things that's ever happened to him. Turning back now wouldn't just mean depriving himself of what is undoubtedly the best sex of his life, but he'd risk losing Becca as a friend, and he can't even imagine his life without her.

After dinner, when his father is locked away in his study and his mother has begged off to go to sleep, Tristan sits in his gigantic room, which is cold despite all the personal touches. He wishes he was back in the city, and he thinks about leaving early, but his mother will be upset if he's not at breakfast in the morning. He can hold out one more day.

He doesn't want to disturb Becca's holiday with her mother, but he needs more than just the *Happy Thanksgiving!*

texts they shared earlier. He pulls out his phone and starts typing.

> *Have a nice dinner?*

She answers right away:

> *It was delicious, but I ate too much. And I wouldn't be upset if I never saw another cranberry again. You?*

Grinning, Tristan types back. He lies:

> *It was great. We didn't have any cranberries though, and now I'm kind of jealous.*

> *Nothing to be jealous over, trust me. If you want though, I'll make you some when I get back home.*

Something about that sentence makes his chest feel warm.

> *Deal. I don't want to keep you from your mom. Have a great time, okay?*

It takes her a while to respond, and when she does, Tristan's certain he'll never be able to wipe the grin off his face:

I will. I miss you.

I miss you too. I'll talk to you tomorrow.

Night.

Goodnight.

CHAPTER
Thirteen

*B*ecca looks down at her phone with a smile on her face as the screen lights up with an incoming text from Tristan. It's just her and her mother sitting at the kitchen table, eating leftover turkey with macaroni and cheese and green beans (no cranberries in sight, thankfully). Becca's mother, Michelle, expects her full time and attention, and isn't a fan of cell phones at the table. Becca knows she's being rude, but she really doesn't care. She feels glued to her phone and doesn't want to miss a single text Tristan sends her, especially when those texts are a little bit dirty and a lot romantic.

Michelle Smith is a romantic at heart, and even though Becca hasn't really mentioned Tristan (she really, really doesn't want to jinx anything), she knows that her mother's onto her. That's probably why she's being so lenient with Becca sitting at the dining room table, checking her phone every 30 seconds during dinner. Becca's surprised that Michelle manages to last nearly a day and a half before asking Becca why she's constantly checking her phone.

"New man?" Michelle says with a knowing smile as she lifts her wine flute up to her lips.

Becca grins and even though she tries to fight the blush, she feels it creeping up her neck into her cheeks. Should she deny it? No, just the thought of that makes her stomach sink.

"Very new," she says.

"Why haven't I heard about him?" Even though Michelle tries to hide it, Becca hears the hurt in her voice.

Becca shares everything with her mother, but she didn't share this latest relationship development, with good reason. Truth is, Michelle *has* heard of Tristan; Becca told her everything about what happened at the beach house after Abby and Cole's wedding. That's precisely why she didn't tell her mother anything about this newest development with Tristan: her mother doesn't exactly have a high opinion of him.

Becca's also wondering if she'd be better off playing this off as a date, nothing serious. Not that Becca thinks things with Tristan are ever going to get serious. Tristan doesn't do serious. *Ever*. Becca knows this; she doesn't want to let herself hope that she'll be different. Still, she knows what she's getting into.

Should she tell her mother what's going on?

What the hell, she thinks.

"You have heard of him," Becca finally answers, sliding a

macaroni noodle onto one of the tines of her fork.

"I have? I don't remember." Her mom shakes her head, her fine blonde bob brushing her shoulders.

Becca puts down her fork and takes a sip of wine. "You have," she replies before taking a deep breath. "It's Cole's friend Tristan."

Michelle's wide blue eyes go wide and her mouth forms this cute little "oh." She's never been one to tell Becca what to do, and she's never been too nosy when it comes to Becca's love life. Becca knows that Michelle only has her best interests at heart, and doesn't want to see her baby girl get hers broken. That's why Becca spends Michelle's protracted silence preparing herself for whatever she's going to say next.

"You seem happy, and I like seeing you happy," Michelle tells her as she reaches out and clasps Becca's hand. "I want to keep seeing you happy, baby. Don't let that boy break your heart."

"He's changed, Mom." Becca can practically see the concentration it takes for Michelle not to roll her eyes. "It was just a misunderstanding we had that night. We became friends, and now…"

"Now what?"

Becca shrugs. "I don't know," she replies quietly. "It's new."

Michelle smiles at her daughter. "I know, you just said. How new is it?"

Looking at the ceiling, Becca thinks about her answer. "Oh, about forty-six hours new, give or take."

"And you still managed to make it home for Thanksgiving."

Michelle smiles, letting Becca know she's just teasing.

"I knew it was important to you. I wanted to be here, Mom. He wanted to make sure I got here, too. He even offered to let me use his jet."

Something shifts in Michelle's expression, from teasing to understanding. "I guess it's too early for him to invite you over to spend Thanksgiving with his family, huh?"

"Things with his family are kind of strained at the moment."

"Things are always strained with people like that."

The words prickle at Becca's skin. She doesn't like her mother's tone or the implication of her words. "What do you mean, 'people like that?'"

"I've read about his family in magazines, Rebecca. I know they're not the nicest, most stable bunch."

Becca really doesn't want to fight with her mother, but she can't let this one pass without saying something.

"Mom, Dad left us, and there was no small amount of trauma in that breakup before he finally took off. If we had enough notoriety for people to care about our lives, we'd be in the tabloids too. And the gossip wouldn't be any better than it is about Tristan's family. People would be saying the same thing about us."

Michelle sighs; Becca hopes that's because she realizes that she's right. "Sweetie, I just don't want you to get hurt."

"Mom," Becca says with a smile. "My eyes are open this time. I know what I'm getting into."

Michelle nods. "I know you know how to take care of yourself. I just worry."

"And I love you for it," Becca replies, squeezing her mom's hand. "I'm only here for a couple of days, and I don't want us to fight about this. Especially because, like I said, it's all so new. Maybe it won't wind up being anything."

Michelle reaches over and cups Becca's cheek. "Oh, honey. I can tell by the look on your face that it's something. It's definitely something."

Shortly after Michelle goes to bed, Becca calls Abby. She and Cole are visiting his family for the holiday, and even though Becca knows that Abby loves them all dearly, she also knows that sometimes Abby needs a little break from them. This seems like as good a time as any.

Becca's proven right when Abby answers on the first ring.

"Hey," Abby says.

"Hey! How are things going?"

"Oh," Abby sighs. "You know how Olivia is, so of course dinner was perfect. Cole's dad took off to the office, so there's a little bit of tension there right now. The kids had fun and everyone's sleeping, so there's that. How's your mom? I meant to call earlier, but dinner took longer than I thought it would and I know she likes to go to bed early, so I wasn't sure…"

"She's doing well. She asked about you. I gave her the chocolate you sent and the gift card which she of course thought was way too generous."

"She knows I can never repay her," Abby says fondly.

"Good thing she's not looking for repayment. She loves you, Abs. And she loves Cole, even though she's starting to resent him for taking you away from her on all the major family holidays."

"Tell her we'll come and visit soon. Actually, I'll call her tomorrow and tell her myself."

"She'll love that," Becca says. Then she takes a deep breath, unsure how to broach the subject that she specifically called to talk about.

"What's up, Beck?"

"Nothing up," she replies, lying through her teeth.

"Uh-huh. I know you. Something's up."

"There's something I want to tell you, but you can't freak out. You can't freak out and you can't tell Cole, okay? Those are the two conditions I must insist on before I tell you what I called to tell you."

"You and Tristan had sex."

"What?" Becca exclaims. "No! Well, yes, we did. But... how did you know that? Did Tristan tell Cole?"

"No," Abby laughs. "Not that I know of. Maybe he's like you and wants to be super secret squirrel about it."

Becca balks. "I'm not trying to be super secret squirrel about it, I just wanted to keep it quiet for now, until I know what's happening. I had to tell you, though."

"You guys haven't talked about things yet?"

"No." Becca picks at a loose thread on her pajama pants. "We had sex and I slept over, and the very next morning I left and came home for Thanksgiving."

"I'm surprised he didn't come with you."

"What do you mean?"

Abby waits a beat, then two, driving Becca absolutely crazy.

"He's got it bad, Becca."

"Oh, please." Despite the rapid acceleration of her heartbeat and the desire to believe what her friend is telling her, Becca just can't. Not yet.

"If denying it makes you feel better, by all means. But I'm telling you, he's got it bad."

"I thought you said he didn't tell Cole!"

"He didn't."

"What?" Becca is so confused.

"He didn't tell Cole. He told me."

Oh. *Oh.* "Why did he…oh, and he told you and I didn't."

"You did, it just took you longer. And I think he told me because he really wants to make sure he doesn't screw it up this time. He assumed you'd already mentioned it and wanted to let me know that he was serious."

Serious? Wow. "You didn't let him know that I hadn't said anything, did you?" If he knew she'd kept it to herself and that he told Abby before Becca did, he might get the wrong idea. He might think she was ashamed of him, or worse.

"No, of course not."

Becca lets out a sigh of relief. "Good. That's good."

"Seems like he's not the only one who's got it bad," she says in her most annoying sing-song voice.

"I'm going to hang up now, Abby."

Abby laughs. "Okay, but we're not done talking about this."

"Don't I know it."

"Love you," Abby says softly.

"Love you back."

Phone still cradled in her hand, Becca falls into a deep, restful sleep.

CHAPTER
Fourteen

The Sunday Becca's due back, Tristan tracks her flight progress from an app on his phone, checking every few minutes to see if she's any closer to home, any closer to *him*. They spoke last night and made plans to meet up for dinner tonight, but Tristan knows he can't wait that long to see her. When he asked her how she planned on getting home from the airport, she told him she was just going to take a cab. Tristan didn't argue with her at the time, because he was planning on surprising her at the airport.

Tristan meets Becca at baggage claim, and the smile she gives him when she sees him standing there is so incredibly worth it.

She runs at him and he swoops her up in his arms, kissing her for all she's worth. He should care that they're in public, but he doesn't. He should care that any and everyone could be taking their picture, but he doesn't care about that either. He just lets himself get wrapped up in the feel of her lips on his and the way her hair smells and the warmth of her body, and he's happy.

It's only been four days, and he's missed her like crazy. It actually makes him nervous how much he missed her, because in a lifetime of flings and short-term relationships, he's never let himself get attached to anyone long enough to actually *miss* them.

"Missed you," Tristan says between pecks. The words just slip out, but he doesn't regret saying them. He's not afraid to let her know that she means something to him, something that's growing bigger and bigger each day.

"I missed you, too," she says, smiling. "I'm glad you're here."

"I couldn't wait until dinner time, is that weird?"

Becca laughs. "No, it's perfect. I didn't want to wait until later either."

"We can go to my place," he says as he grabs her bag off of the luggage carousel and leads her toward the door. "Have dessert first."

"Which place? Your place, or your off-limits-until-you're-all-grown-up place with the super soft bed?"

"My place has a super soft bed, too," he tells her. "I think we should christen it."

Her cheeks turn a glorious shade of pink as she tries and fails to fight a smile. "That sounds good."

"Oh," he assures her, picking up his pace. "It will be."

As they cruise down the expressway toward Manhattan, Tristan's really kicking himself for not bringing his driver. He and Becca could be stretched out in the backseat of his town car right now, doing unspeakable things to each other. But no, he had to be an idiot and drive them himself. Lesson learned for the next time, he thinks.

Seems like Becca's regretting the lack of a backseat all to themselves, too. She's got her hand on his thigh, and it's inching further up as they drive. Her head is resting on his shoulder, and occasionally she turns and presses a kiss to his neck. Sometimes it's soft and lingering, sometimes she sucks a little and eases the sting with her tongue. He strains almost unbearably against the tight confines of his jeans, mentally calculating how much longer they'll be in this goddamn car. He can just drop the keys off with the doorman to park, rush inside the building and press Becca up against the wall of the elevator.

As if Becca can read his mind and knows how desperate he is to get her naked, she decides to torture him a little by running her palm along his erection. His hips shift up into the warmth of her hand, like they have a mind of their own.

Tristan takes his eyes off of the road for a split second, to shoot Becca a warning look.

"Don't start something you're not going to finish," he says, his voice almost a growl.

"Oh," she replies, pressing harder against him. "I fully

intend on finishing it."

If Tristan presses the accelerator a little harder, no one would blame him.

"Tell me what you want," Becca says, her voice all breathy and full of need.

"I want you to suck my cock." Tristan's never talked dirty to Becca before, and what better time to test the waters than when they're both standing naked in the middle of his bedroom, hands and mouths all over each other's bodies?

If he had any worries about how that would go over, he finds they're completely unfounded when he gets a look at Becca's face. She's almost…*eager*, and Tristan knows this woman is going to be the death of him.

She slides her fingernails down the ridges of his abs as she drops to her knees right in front of him, her wavy blonde hair tumbling over her shoulders. She looks at him with half-hooded eyes, and he tenderly brushes a strand of hair off of her forehead. She closes her eyes and presses a kiss against his hip, making his cock twitch in anticipation of her mouth. She runs her hands up and down his thighs, building him up as her mouth roams across his abdomen and lower, her lips pretty much everywhere but where he wants them the most. She's such a tease, and he loves it. Luckily, she wants to bring him to the edge of his senses, not torture him, so the teasing doesn't last too long.

She licks a stripe from the bottom of his shaft to the tip as she cups his balls, gently giving them a tug. His fingers slide through her hair as his head falls back, losing himself in sensation. He holds it together pretty well as she licks and sucks and strokes him, but his knees go a little weak when he looks down and sees her smiling at him as she laves the tip of his cock with her tongue. When she closes her lips around him and takes him fully in her mouth, he thinks he could die like this and be happy about it. It's not until he hits the back of her throat as she swallows that he reaches his limit and has to pull away.

Becca looks up at him, adorably confused.

"What did I-"

Tristan hooks his hands beneath her arms and pulls her up until she's crushed against his chest. He leans down and kisses her, then lifts her.

"You're perfect," Tristan says. It's not really an answer, but it's true just the same, and when Becca wraps her legs around his waist, he carries her over to his bed and sets her down on the edge. Somehow she knows exactly what he wants, so she lays back and spreads her legs for him.

Tristan runs his hands along the insides of her thighs. God, she's so wet for him.

He doesn't waste any time, they've been teasing each other for the better part of two hours. He aches to taste her, so he leans in and goes straight for her clit, loving the way her whole body tenses and relaxes at his touch. He licks her, running his tongue along her slit and back up, circling and sucking. He can't get enough of her taste, can't get enough of the way she feels around his tongue. Between soft moans that get louder the longer he goes on, she slides her fingers through his hair, tugging on the ends, urging him faster, harder.

"You taste so good," he tells her.

Becca lifts herself up on her elbows and looks down at him, eyes hooded. Tristan's struck by how beautiful she is like this, all spread out for him, breathless and on the verge of coming apart. She makes this noise low and in the back of her throat, and Tristan slides his fingers inside of her, crooking them up until they hit just the right spot. Becca keens as she rocks against Tristan's hand, and he does his best to drive her over the edge with his tongue.

"More, please. I…"

"Like this?" he asks, pumping harder, faster. Whatever she wants, he'll do it.

She gently presses on the back of his head, guiding his mouth back to her clit, and she shivers as she grinds against him. In no time at all, she's crying out as she comes on his tongue.

Maybe this makes him a selfish bastard, but he doesn't even give her time to ride out her pleasure. He's so hard and aching for her, he slips on a condom and slides into her right away. They both let out ragged breaths, and Tristan stills; he can still feel the contractions from her orgasm.

"You make me feel so good," Becca says. She looks flushed and happy, and somewhere in a non-lust-addled area of Tristan's brain, he's wondering if she's talking about more than the orgasm he just gave her.

"I'm about to make you feel better," Tristan replies, giving her a sly smile as he rotates his hips.

Becca's eyes briefly flutter shut, but then her gaze is focused solely on him. "Put your back into it."

Without a doubt, a bossy Becca is a real turn on for him. So, he does as she asks and he puts his back into it. He puts everything he has into it. The first night they spent together was slow and sweet and exploratory. This time it's all need and want and desire. Their kisses are desperate, full of tongues and teeth and nipping lips as Tristan pounds into her, relentlessly pushing them both to the brink of pleasure.

Just when he's beginning to lose himself, Tristan feels Becca press on his shoulder.

"Roll over," she says. He does.

Becca straddles him, hair wild and skin splotchy from all the places he's left his mark on her. Tristan loves this position; he's got unrestricted access to any place on her body he wants to touch, and he wants to touch it all. He brings his hands to her breasts, feeling the soft fullness beneath his fingers. He pinches her nipples as she rides him. She threads her fingers through his and brings their hands down to the mattress, pressing against it and using them for leverage as she leans in for a kiss.

Tristan licks into her mouth, overtaken by the taste of her. He's going to come. Now. He can't hold it off any longer.

He untangles his fingers from hers and brings his hand down between them, rubbing her clit with his thumb as he thrusts up into her. She's breathing hard, eyes closed and mouth dropped open, and all he wants to do is make her feel as good as he does.

"You gonna come?" he asks.

"Yes," she breaths, eyes screwed up tight. "Yeah."

Tristan sits up and pulls one of her breasts into his mouth, pulling her nipple between his teeth, knowing that'll get her off. One tug and one thrust are all it takes to undo her, and she's squeezing around him, pulling him into his own orgasm. They ride it out together, and Becca collapses into his chest as they both try catching their breath.

"You're amazing," Becca says, pressing a kiss against his pec.

Tristan laughs and gathers her hair at the nape of her neck. "I was just about to say the same thing about you." His fingertips run a circuit up and down her spine. The relaxing rhythm makes her fall asleep in no time, and Tristan's not too far behind.

CHAPTER
Fifteen

Over the next few weeks, waking up with Tristan's arms wrapped around her becomes commonplace for Becca. It's something she could get used to pretty easily, snuggling up against his warm body, feeling safe and secure. She's trying to keep her mind from going there, because she's pretty sure this is just a friends-with-benefits kind of situation, and she doesn't want to fall too hard. All signs point to him wanting to change, but his track record hasn't been a good one, and guys like him don't usually go from fucking models to fucking girls like her on a permanent basis. She's pretty sure she's just a pit stop on a road to something else, and she's okay with it.

Well, she's trying to be okay with it.

Her rational mind tells her that he came to pick her up from the airport yesterday because they have great sex and he was horny, and he knew it would be a sure thing. The not-so-rational mind thinks about the way he looks at her, the way he makes her feel, and she has difficulty imagining that this could ever be temporary. She knows he wants to change, but it's the kind of thing where the idea of it is really, really good. Maybe he's having fun with her, maybe he's just doing a trial run of being responsible and domestic, but one day he'll realize that it's not as fun and glamorous as the life he used to live, and she'll wake up and find out that he took off again, like that night at the beach house.

Part of her knows she's not being fair, that she should give him the benefit of the doubt. But the other part—the part that's desperately trying to avoid a broken heart—is just waiting for the other shoe to drop, and with Tristan's track record she realizes that shoe will drop sooner rather than later. She puts that out of her mind as much as she can, though, because she's having too much fun just being with him.

Sometimes they spend the night at her house, sometimes they spend the night at his. Becca prefers staying at his place because it's nicer (and also because he has a chef who makes the most delicious omelets every morning for breakfast). Tristan's place is also closer to Becca's office; she only has to take one train, and she actually has time to eat those delicious omelets before she leaves.

It only takes a few days for Tristan to realize that if his driver takes her to work, she gets to stay in bed for an extra 15 minutes.

She doesn't take the train much after that.

They haven't had a talk about what they are, and there are no labels. They just continue on as friendly as they always were, but now they have sex. Lots and lots of sex. And there's also the whole sleeping together (literally) thing. Becca doesn't push the issue because she's happy with the way things are, and she's afraid that if she asks him to define them, he'll give her an answer she doesn't want to hear. Tristan doesn't bring it up either, probably because he doesn't want to tell her what he knows she doesn't want to hear.

Not mentioning it keeps up the status quo. Becca likes the status quo.

Becca meets a few of Tristan's friends when they're out to dinner or walking through Midtown, but only a *few*. She gets the feeling that he's purposely avoiding most of the people he spent time with before he and Becca got together, probably because they seem like the type to encourage one-night stands with models and partying at every opportunity. She doesn't get the sense that Tristan misses any of that, really, but she wonders how long that will last.

He spends more and more time with Cole. Cole, the kind of man she knows Tristan can be, the kind of man she knows Tristan is trying to be: dedicated and loving and responsible. She wonders how much he actually *wants* that, though. Regardless, Tristan's really good at making Becca feel wanted. When doubt creeps up on her and settles in her skin, and she starts to wonder if maybe she should break things off and get out before she's in too deep, one smile or wink from Tristan is all it takes to wash everything away.

It always creeps back in, though, and Becca tries to

remember his apology for the way he treated her. She promised herself that she would leave what happened between them at Abby and Cole's wedding in the past. He said he was sorry, and it's not fair to hold that against him. Still, she wishes it was easier to forget.

In an effort to mend the rocky relationship he has with his father and end the argument about Tristan's business future, he and Becca work on a plan for him to expand his nightclub ownership and turn it into something more than a hobby by branching out into other entertainment venues. They do research, and Tristan hires a consultant to help him expand on his ideas. Tristan doesn't seem as engaged in it as Becca thinks he should be, like he's going through the motions to appease his father without having to get in on the family business.

She knows she should say something, but she doesn't. Like a lot of things where Tristan's concerned, she's afraid that talking about it will bring everything crashing down. She's happy now, living in her house of cards.

CHAPTER
Sixteen

*A*nother Wednesday, and Tristan is sitting in his father's office in an uncomfortable suit and tie, feeling more out of place than he ever thought possible. Things between him and Clay still aren't good at all, and he doesn't expect that they'll get any better after today. At the end of this meeting, his father is going to needle him about taking over, and Tristan's still going to resist. He's not even sure why he still shows up for these meetings, apart from the fact that some part of him is worried that this is the one thread that is still keeping them together. As long as his father is still badgering him about the company, he still cares a little. As long as he still cares a little, Tristan has a chance at changing his mind.

Clay thinks that Tristan is allergic to responsibility, that he doesn't want to take over the company because he doesn't want anything tying him down. That might've been a little bit true at one point, but even though he hasn't been with Becca all that long, he finds himself craving things he never thought he wanted before. Responsibility is one of those things.

Tristan knows that a man without any drive, who spends his time investing in nightclubs but never actually building anything tangible, isn't the kind of guy he wants to be for her. He wants to give her the nine-to-five guy, the one who's gainfully employed in a position that actually means something. He just doesn't know what that *is* yet. Sometimes he thinks he could search his whole life for it and never figure it out.

What he does know is that his future isn't in this company, sitting behind a huge mahogany desk in a corner office with a great view of the city, spending his days trying to ease investor worries. So, he's trying his hand at something new. He's planning. He's going to expand his club business, branch out into restaurants and other entertainment venues.

He's working on a portfolio now, and he's going to present it to his father over Christmas. Maybe that will appease Clay for now. Maybe that will give Tristan a little bit of breathing room.

When the conference call is finally over, Clay leans back in his chair and drums his fingertips along the top of his desk. Sitting in the chair across from him, every muscle in Tristan's body tightens. This is exactly the same pose Clay would sit in whenever he was delivering bad news. Being sent to a new boarding school? Fingers drumming on the desk. Grandmother's in a coma? Fingers drumming on the desk.

Fingers drumming on the desk.

Tristan braces himself for the blow.

To his surprise, there's no yelling. There's no talk about how much Tristan has disappointed him, about how he needs to grow up, about how he needs to take over the business.

Instead, Clay pulls open his top desk drawer, pulls out a thick white envelope, and slides it across the desk.

Tristan reaches for it, trying to hide the hesitation he's feeling and failing miserably. He also fails at hiding his trepidation; the very last thing he wants to be right now is an open book.

"What's this?" Tristan asks.

"Open it and find out," Clay says with all the ruthlessness he usually displays when he's closing a deal.

Tristan slides his finger under the flap and pulls out the papers inside. He unfolds them, and he doesn't have to read too far down to understand exactly what these papers are for. Really, this shouldn't shock him as much as it does, but he feels a cold rising fear welling up inside of him that's quickly replaced by white-hot anger.

"You're disinheriting me?" he asks. He manages to sound a lot less hurt and angry than he feels.

"Perceptive," Clay replies, like an absolute asshole.

"Just because I don't want to take over the business?"

Clay nods, and the sheer coldness in his eyes makes Tristan uneasy. "You're not living up to the potential I expect from you."

"You mean I'm not living up to being the kind of son you

want. I'm not letting you control my life like I'm some kind of employee."

"Since I'll no longer be paying you," Clay says coldly, "you won't be under my employ, so you can feel free to do whatever you like, provided you can pay for it."

"So that's it," Tristan says bitterly.

"What more should there be?"

"I thought for sure you'd try to manipulate me into doing what you want, use something I care about as leverage."

"You don't care about anything enough for me to use as leverage," Clay says coldly. "Is that what you want? To be manipulated?"

"No," Tristan replies, tapping the envelope on his knee. The repetitive motion soothes him, keeps him from flying right off the handle. "I wanted you to have some faith in me. Just once, just a little."

"What's there to have faith in?"

Sometimes it kills Tristan, how businesslike his father can be. When he gets distant like this, Tristan wonders what on earth his mother ever saw in him, wonders how any woman could love him enough to marry him. To start a family with him.

"I'm working on something."

"What, more nightclubs? More nonsense? Tristan," he says, sitting up and resting his forearms on his desk. "I'm talking about something that has weight to it, something you can be proud to put our family name on. I will say that I'm surprised that you've managed to stay out of the papers for a few weeks, but everyone has a dry spell. Even you."

"It's not a dry spell," Tristan says defensively.

"You'll be back at it before long," Clay replies. "Trust me, I know you."

"Not this time, Dad." Tristan is vehement about this.

"Why not?"

He swallows, not wanting to admit this to his father in a fight. This is the type of thing he was worried about his father using to manipulate him. New as it is, *this* is his thing worth being manipulated for. "I've met someone." He doesn't tell Clay Becca's name, even though Clay could find it if he really wanted to know.

"And what a catch she's landed," Clay replies snidely. "I bet you're just what her parents always dreamed of her bringing home, an unemployed rich guy. Wait, knowing how you pick 'em, it probably is. I'm sure your bank account is a big draw for her. *Was* a big draw."

Seething anger pushes Tristan to his feet, and he pounds on his father's desk, demanding his attention. "You do *not* talk about her like that. She doesn't care about my money."

Clay's mouth twists into an unsettling grin. "Tell me that once she realizes that you don't have any."

Tristan tries desperately to shake off his old insecurities. He knows he's worth more than his checkbook to Becca. He knows she doesn't care about his money, but he can't shake the dreaded feeling that accompanies the 'what if's.

"She's different," Tristan says, sounding not at all sure about that.

"They're all different, until they're not."

"What's that supposed to mean?" He thinks his panic

must be evident on his face because his father actually looks like he's taking pity on him.

Sitting back in his chair, Clay gives Tristan a shrewd, apprising look. After what seems like forever, he finally speaks. "Tell you what," he says, reaching out for the envelope. Tristan hands it to him. "You want me to make a deal with you?"

Tristan swallows, but doesn't manage an answer.

Clay holds the envelope up. "You have one month. Get your shit together Tristan, and if in a month you can show me a plan, tell me what you're going to do with the rest of your goddamn life, as long as I approve of it I'll rip up these papers. Give me something to go off of, make an effort at *something,* and we'll talk."

Tristan's completely numb, but he manages to nod. He should tell his father to take his money and go fuck himself with it, but he doesn't.

They're all different, until they're not, plays on a loop in his head.

If Becca's not different, he doesn't want to find out.

"You're just going to walk past your own mother without saying a word?"

Tristan turns, surprised to find his mother staring back at him, looking a little bit hurt. He shouldn't be so surprised to see her, given that they're standing in the lobby of a building that bears their last name.

"Mom," Tristan says, leaning in for a hug. "What are you doing here?"

"I'm meeting your father for lunch. What's the matter?" she asks, concern clouding her eyes. She never can turn off that damned motherly instinct that always puts her so in touch with his emotions.

"I just had a talk with dad."

Her eyes narrow. "About?"

Tristan looks around, not wanting to say the words in a lobby full of people employed by his father. That makes this more humiliating somehow, although he's not quite sure why. When he doesn't answer, his mother gently leads him over to a secluded area of the lobby.

"Tristan. Talk."

"He's disinheriting me."

Charlotte Blackwell takes a deep breath and lets out a long-suffering sigh. "Damn that man."

"He took it back at the last minute. He told me he'd give me a month to come up with a plan." She rubs her hands together and looks up at the ceiling. When she turns back toward him, her eyes bright, he knows he's not going to like what she has to say next.

"What?" he asks warily.

"Come to the house next weekend and spend Saturday night."

Tristan's confused. "Okay, but-"

"Bring your girlfriend."

Tristan's eyebrows knit together. "What? How do you

even know about her."

His mother's eyes narrow, and she gives him *the look*. "I'm your mother, of course I know about her. I don't know her name, but I know she exists. I can tell; she's changed you."

"Mom," he warns. "I'm not going to use her in dad's twisted little game to bend me to his will."

"I'm not asking you to," she tells him as she squeezes his hand. "Just trust me. Bring her, let us meet her."

Tristan agrees, although the sinking feeling in his stomach tells him this is a very, very bad idea.

CHAPTER
Seventeen

Becca doesn't know why she agreed to this. She and Tristan have been sleeping together for, like, a month, and she still doesn't know exactly where she stands with him, but when he asked her to come to Connecticut this weekend to meet his parents, she couldn't tell him no. She didn't want to tell him no. She blames it on the fact that he threw the question at her right as she was coming down from a mind-blowing orgasm, and yeah, maybe she has a little morbid curiosity about the kind of family life Tristan has.

So, here she is, sitting in the passenger seat of his BMW, twisting her hands nervously in her lap as she tries to stave off the nerves that are making her stomach roll. Tristan's got some classic rock anthem playing on what has to be a premium sound system, but all Becca can keep thinking about is why she's in this car on her way to meet his parents. His *parents*. She's only met the parents in two relationships, and those were *months* old before that happened. Becca and Tristan's relationship is still in its infant stages. It can't even hold its head up.

No, she's not going to think about this too much. She's not going to doubt it, or wonder what the hurry is. She's in the car, she's already committed, so she's just going to enjoy herself and let what happens happen. That's the best way to deal with the nerves, she thinks.

"You okay?" Tristan asks.

If Becca didn't know any better, she'd think that Tristan was pretty nervous himself, but he's focusing on her nerves so that's nice. She doesn't want him to think she doesn't want to meet his parents, and she really doesn't want him to know the underlying reasons why she's nervous about doing just that. The "too far too fast" conversation seems too late at this point, considering they're already in Connecticut. Then there's the fact that if Becca comes out on the other side of this weekend with Tristan's parents not liking her, that could be the end of things anyway. Or the beginning of the end, at least. She's not ready for that yet.

"Becca?" Tristan's looking at her with a soft, amused smile.

"Yeah?"

"I asked if you were okay?"

"Yeah, I'm good. I'm just...I don't know." Just say it, Becca. "I'm a little nervous."

"Don't be. They're going to love you," he replies. She

tries not to think about how tightly he's gripping the steering wheel when he says it. His knuckles are white.

Becca nods, and her mind starts racing. Will he be expecting her to introduce him to her mother? She never even considered that, and is suddenly thankful that she's going home for Christmas next week. If her mother was coming to New York, she'd have a whole other set of problems on her hands, and she'd be even more nervous than she already is.

Breathe Becca, she thinks. *Just breathe.*

She takes slow, relaxing breaths and loses herself in the snow-covered hills they pass as they speed down the highway. Anything to stave off the panic that's rising inside of her the closer they get to the Blackwell home.

As if he can sense her reluctance, Tristan takes Becca's hand and brings the back of it to his lips, planting a soft kiss there.

"They're going to love you," he repeats.

It sounds a whole lot like he's trying to convince himself, too.

Charlotte Blackwell is refined and elegant in a way that absolutely does not put Becca at ease. She has a very "don't touch anything because I don't want your fingerprints all over it" kind of way about her that makes the awkward hug she gives Becca when Tristan introduces them even *more* awkward. Becca's seen Tristan's mother in countless photo spreads (hers were actually posed for and published in reputable publications, unlike most of her son's), but she's even fancier than Becca expected, and that makes Becca's nerves spike off the charts.

Standing in the gargantuan foyer of what can only be described as the Blackwell castle (seriously, this place is huge, like an American Versailles), Becca eyes Charlotte nervously. She's standing there in an elegant red dress with her hands clasped in front of her. She looks like a queen, and the red she's wearing pops out among all the Christmas decorations. There are wreaths and ribbons everywhere, and a grand tree wrapped in white lights and gold ornaments at the base of the stairway. It's a far cry from the construction paper Christmas trees she and her mom used to make when she was a kid, and Becca's surprised to find she would actually prefer that. This place could use a little personality, and despite the decorations, it felt completely devoid of happiness.

No wonder Tristan didn't want to come alone.

"It's very nice to meet you, Rebecca," Tristan's mother says.

"It's nice to meet you as well, and please, call me Becca."

Charlotte grins at her and glances over at Tristan before she says, "I've heard so much about you."

Tristan, for his part, looks incredibly uncomfortable. Becca begins to wonder if Charlotte's lying about hearing about her at all.

"Where's Dad?" Tristan asks. It's difficult to miss the undercurrent of anger in his voice.

"In the study," Charlotte replies. "He'll be down in time

for dinner." The look Charlotte gives her son is loaded; Becca has no idea what's passing between them, although Tristan seems to get it just fine. The air shifts around them. Becca can practically feel Tristan tensing, so she turns and gives him a smile, hoping that will calm him. It seems to work.

"Tristan, why don't you take Becca upstairs and show her your room? I'll have your things brought up later." Charlotte says.

"Okay." Tristan laces his fingers through Becca's, then stops and drops a kiss on his mother's cheek.

Tristan's room is *insane*. Rich wood furniture, ornate moulding, lush fabrics on his bed. There are actual paintings on the wall, which surprises Becca. Not that she was expecting a poster of a mostly-naked woman covered in suds and draped over a sports car, but paintings? What on earth was that like as a kid?

"Is this the room you had when you were growing up?" Becca asks as she looks around, taking it all in. The sitting area, the fireplace, it's just…too much.

Tristan nods as he sits on the edge of his bed. "Not what you were expecting?"

"Not really. I cannot imagine this place with, like, hanging mobiles and toy cars and stuff a kid likes in it."

"I had some kid stuff in our penthouse in the city, but not really here. I didn't get to play all that much when I was younger, things were different for me."

"Different for you how?"

Tristan sighs and looks around. "Lonely," he replies with a sad smile. "I read a lot and was involved in a lot of sports and after school stuff, but I didn't really have very many friends apart from Cole. When I was really young, I played with the housekeeper's kids, but my parents put an end to that. My dad sent me off to boarding school when I was twelve, and I didn't make it back here all that often after that. I made friends and spent time with them. My only saving grace was that Cole's father sent him there, too."

Money, Becca thinks. *It fucks you up.* She wishes she could've given Tristan the kind of childhood that she had, where his mom would've brought snacks after soccer games, and he could've ruined his best pants with grass marks from skidding during recess. If only she could turn back time, take him from this place and show him what it was like to really be a kid.

"Are you okay sleeping in here with me?" he asks.

Becca walks over and cups his cheek, slides her thumb across his cheekbone, and gives him a soft, sweet smile. "I wouldn't want to be anywhere else." She leans down and presses a kiss to his lips, desperate to break this air of melancholy around him. She wants him to snap out of it, to wake up, to be the guy she's used to him being when they're not in this place.

Becca drapes her arms around Tristan's neck, and he slides his hands up and down her thighs. "You okay?"

Tristan nods, pressing his forehead against her belly.

"I'm glad you're here."

She crooks her fingers underneath his chin and lifts his head so she can kiss him. "Me too."

Becca really doesn't like to pass judgment on people she's just met, but she's fairly comfortable in her opinion that Clay Blackwell is an asshole. He shows up to dinner late, after Becca, Tristan and Tristan's mother have already started eating, and apparently this is normal behavior for him. What kills her the most about this is that she can see Tristan's anxiety rise the later his father is. Tristan, for all the care-free attitude that he presents to the world, is someone who cares very much, especially about what his father thinks of him. Becca's certain that he wants Clay's approval desperately.

She's also certain that Clay is well aware of this, and is very judicious of every single action he takes around his son. Like an asshole.

Clay doesn't even bother introducing himself to Becca, and she has to bite back the vicious words that are dancing right along the end of her tongue, just wanting to come out. She doesn't want to be rude to this man in his own home, and she doesn't want to add to the stress that Tristan is so obviously feeling about this situation.

"Darling," Charlotte says as she folds her hands in front of her. "This is Tristan's Becca."

Becca just wants to crawl into a hole and die. She and

Tristan haven't had the boyfriend/girlfriend conversation, and hearing his mother introduce her this way makes her stomach swoop. She doesn't say anything, but she does look over at Tristan, who is looking at her intently.

"It's a pleasure to meet you," Becca says, starting to stand awkwardly. She only makes it a quarter of the way out of her seat before she realizes how rude they must think she is; what, was she going to shake his hand across the table? Ultimately it doesn't matter, because Clay just offers Becca a short, insincere smile before he turns his attention back to his food.

Tristan looks absolutely mortified, and Becca thinks he might be getting ready to tell her they're going to leave when his mother starts talking.

"So Becca," Charlotte says, her voice kind as she looks at her asshole husband. "What do you do for a living? Where is your family from?"

Becca puts down her soup spoon and straightens her back, as if her posture is going to stop her from worrying about Charlotte Blackwell judging her.

"I'm an account manager at an advertising firm in Midtown, and I grew up in Ohio, just outside of Columbus."

Tristan is sitting all the way over on the other side of the table, too far for her to reach out and touch, but she feels his foot bump against hers. She's glad for it, too, when she sees Charlotte gaping for a moment, before she schools her expression. Did Tristan not tell them anything at all about her? A nervous rush fizzles out into her fingertips, because why on earth would he bring her into this situation without preparing them for the fact that Becca is not the society girl they were probably expecting him to bring home. She knows that Tristan isn't embarrassed of her, and she also knows that he doesn't think anything about their income or "class" differences, but it would've been nice if he'd prepared his mother for the fact that he was bringing home a nobody who grew up in Podunk, Ohio.

"And your parents? What business are they in?"

Becca gets the sense that Charlotte expects her to be ashamed of her mother, so Becca holds her head up high and says, "My mother is an office manager. I don't know what my father does. I haven't spoken to him in a very long time."

Charlotte nods satisfactorily, as if that's exactly what she was expecting to hear from Becca, and Becca has to work quickly to hide the flash of anger she feels.

"What's the name of the firm you work for?" Charlotte asks. She feels like this is a job interview rather than a dinner with the parents of…well, the guy she's sleeping with.

"Dalton and McKinnon," Becca says pleasantly. It sounds forced to Becca's own ears, but she doesn't think Charlotte notices.

"Clay, are you familiar?" Charlotte asks.

Clay finally looks up from his soup and gives Becca a look that makes her want to disappear. "Never heard of it," he replies.

Dalton and McKinnon is one of the most prestigious firms in the city. Clay Blackwell is an asshole *and* a liar. Tristan shoots her a sympathetic look, and she dips her spoon in her bowl, determined to make it through the rest of this dinner.

134

The first time Becca feels comfortable in the Blackwell home is when she and Tristan are in their pajamas, and his body is wrapped around hers in his soft, soft bed. She's using his chest as a pillow, and luckily Tristan doesn't seem to mind. She turns her head and kisses his skin, hoping to start something more, because she wants to give him a physical outlet to relieve some of his tension. Somewhere in the back of her mind she wonders if this is part of the reason he invited her: for emotional and physical companionship. She imagines he gets pretty lonely when he's here, even now as an adult.

Becca plants kisses all across Tristan's chest, and he continues to rub a steady circuit up and down her back, never progressing things past what Becca would consider the "light petting" phase.

"You drive me crazy," Tristan says before planting a kiss at the crown of Becca's head. "But I just can't tonight."

Becca feels the slightest twinge of disappointment, but she quickly pushes it away. She was kind of expecting him to rebuff her.

"It's okay," she says, snuggling against him. "I just wanted to make you feel better."

"You make me feel better," he whispers into her hair.

"This place…it's so not you."

"What do you mean?"

Becca shrugs, looking at the ornate, over-the-top

everything that decorates this room. "You're not chandeliers and Victorian furniture, you're a big screen TV and the comfiest couch I've ever sat on. You're feet-on-the-coffee table. You're...*you.* It never made sense to me why you had this fancy penthouse on 5th Avenue that you rarely visit, despite the *incredible* view; now it makes sense. It's like you're saving it until you have a grown-up life where you'll deserve it, when you deserve it now. You just need to make it *you.*" Becca lets out a long, drawn-out breath. "It makes sense in my head."

"It makes sense," he says, smiling. "It makes sense to me."

"Good," she replies, tilting her head up for a kiss. His lips are so soft and warm. "Now let's go to sleep."

"'kay."

"Tristan?"

"Yeah."

"If I get up in the middle of the night and get lost on my way to the bathroom, will you come find me?"

Tristan laughs, and Becca enjoys the rumbly feeling against her cheek. "It's just on the other side of the room."

"I know. It's a long distance trek, and I worry."

"Yeah," he whispers, pressing his lips against her forehead. "I'll find you."

CHAPTER
Eighteen

"I never thought I'd see the day when you would encourage me to put more clothes *on*," Becca says, laughing, as Tristan helps her slip on her thick down coat.

"There's a first time for everything." He presses a kiss against her neck before he lifts up the fur-lined hood and pulls the drawstrings tight.

"Hey!" she laughs, swatting at his hands as she loosens the strings. "It's not that cold outside. I don't need to walk around like we're going on an expedition in Antarctica."

"Maybe we are."

Becca purses her lips, and Tristan can't help himself. He has to lean down and kiss them. She tastes like cherries.

"You need mittens, too," he reminds her.

Becca dramatically slides her hands in her pockets and pulls out a pair, then slips them on her hands. "Happy?"

"Very." He kisses her again.

"Where are we going, anyway? Since I know you're lying about Antarctica."

"We're going for a little walk, that okay? If it's too cold, or-"

"No, it's okay. I grew up in Ohio, remember? I used to put on shorts when it hit sixty degrees. I was made for weather like this. Besides, it's not really that cold out."

"If you do get too cold, let me know and we'll come back to the house, okay?"

"Or one of your servants will come and pick us up on a fancy little golf cart, am I right?"

Tristan laughs, feeling this lightness bubble up in his chest. It's been such a long time since he's been happy being home. Even though he was hesitant about inviting Becca here this weekend, he's so glad he did.

Now, if only he could get his parents to warm up to her. He thinks his dad might be a lost cause; based on the conversation they had in his office about the kind of girls Tristan usually dated, he knows his father walked into the dining room the day he met Becca with a preconceived notion about her. She didn't come from the likes of Blackwell money, therefore her only interest was getting her hands on Tristan's. If he hadn't felt that way when he sat down to dinner, he certainly did once Becca told him that her mother was an office manager and raised Becca by herself.

His mother, though, that's a different story. She doesn't come from a prominent family, so there is some hope with her, and as long as there's hope with her then maybe she can bring Becca into his father's good graces. The truth is, Tristan's not exactly sure how they could be disappointed in her; she's entirely different from the women he used to hook up with, and she's the first woman he's brought home to meet his parents. Even if his father disinherits him, he still would've wanted his mother to meet Becca, and he would've made sure that happened, provided Becca stuck around.

Shaking himself out of his thoughts, Tristan reaches up and makes sure Becca's coat zipper is zipped as high as it can go. "Are we good?"

"We're better than good," she says. She gets this tender look on her face as she gives him this soft smile that she only ever seems to have around him. That smile makes Tristan want to kiss her, so that's exactly what he does.

"What was that for?" Becca asks.

"For being you," he says, leaning in and kissing her. "For making me smile."

"I only ever want to make you smile," she says, and the honesty of it nearly takes his breath away, so he just stands back and stares at her, trying to make sense of the jumbled feelings unfurling in his chest.

"Where are you off to?" Startled, Tristan turns and sees his mother standing a few feet away from them. He didn't even know she'd entered the room. She's dressed more casually than he's seen her in a while, wearing khakis and a sweater, and she's holding her favorite mug.

"We're going for a walk. I wanted to show Becca the grounds."

Tristan notices his mother looking at Becca thoughtfully,

and he's wondering how much of their conversation she overheard. He watches as Charlotte reaches into her sweater pocket and pulls something out, then places it in Becca's outstretched hand.

"Break those packets in half if you get too cold, and they'll warm up your hands, okay? Tristan," she says, looking at him. "You have your phone?"

"Yes mother," he says exasperatedly.

"You'll call if you have any trouble?"

"I will. But we're not going on an expedition, Mom. We're just going for a walk around back."

His mother smiles at him, and it's an honest, real smile. She hasn't smiled like that in a long time."

"You two have fun, okay?"

Becca nods and grins. "We will."

Tristan tries to ignore the burning feeling of his mother's gaze as she watches the two of them walk out the door.

"I don't think she likes me," Becca says, pushing some stray hairs back that have somehow made their way out from under her hood. Tristan has his arm slung around her shoulder, holding her close to his side to keep her warm. There's not a lot of snow on the ground and it's not very windy, so despite the fact that it's the middle of December, the walk is actually fairly pleasant. That probably has at least a little bit to do with the company, he thinks.

"What do you mean?" Tristan asks, even though he knows what she means.

She gives him a look that lets him know exactly that. "They don't like me, I can tell. It's colder in that house than it is out here," she says, giving him a smile that lets him know that she's not offended, just that she's noticed.

"My mom is just…cautious. My dad is…yeah, he's always like that."

"Wow," Becca says under her breath, so quietly Tristan isn't sure he's meant to hear it. She falls out of step with him for a moment as she gets up on her tiptoes and presses a kiss to his cheek.

"What's that for?"

"Being you, even though you grew up with that."

It's nice, having someone who understands. The only other person he's ever talked to about his struggles with his father is Cole, but his viewpoint is skewed, growing up in a household where duty came first. Having had a "normal" childhood and the freedom to choose whatever she wanted to do in life, Becca's opinion makes him feel like he's not so off base for being confused and reluctant to take the reins of his family's business. He can't help but thinking, yet again, how glad he is that Becca learned to make the best of a bad situation when she was growing up. He remembers her telling him about how she had nothing when she was a child, but her mom always managed to make do. It makes him think that maybe if he didn't have the safety of his inheritance, she could teach him how to make do, too. For a fleeting moment he thinks maybe they could be happy together, living like that.

Then he remembers the crushing heaviness of his father's disapproval, and how he'd do anything—*anything*—to be in his good graces, to get his approval just once. He'd even invite the woman he's falling in love with to a weekend getaway without telling her the real reason why she's here: a misguided attempt to appease his father by showing him that he's moved on from his one-night-stand, Vegas showgirl phase. That he's not going to be in the tabloids anymore because he's found a guiding, steady presence in his life.

He needs to tell her all that, but if he can just wait until they get through this weekend, until they're back in the city...

"With your dad the way he is, neglecting his family to hole up in his study and generally being an asshole-"

Tristan gives her a look, surprised that she's being so open with him, but loving it all the same.

Becca shrugs unapologetically. "I'm just saying, I can see why you're hesitant to get involved in the family business if that's what it turns you into. Is this just because you're fighting, or..."

Tristan shakes his head. He wishes his father's attitude was just because they're at an impasse. "No, he's been like that for as long as I can remember."

"God," Becca says, sorrow filling her voice. "My mom? She was always involved in my life. She couldn't get enough of me, it was almost too much. Now I'm here and I see how... never mind."

Tristan looks over at her, because he wants her to keep talking. "What's the matter?"

"Could I be more insensitive? Here I am, talking about how great my mom is when all I can think about is how much I wish you had someone like her in your life when you were growing up. I have nothing but good memories, and you don't. I just wish that you did, that's all. I wish I could give you that."

Tristan pulls her closer into his side. "I have good memories, just not many associated with my family. But it's okay," he says, giving her a squeeze. "That's what the rest of my life is for."

Becca nods and they walk on in silence, until: "So, where exactly are we going? You have a secret hideaway out here?"

"Of sorts," Tristan replies, pointing at their destination a few yards away.

"This is like something out of a horror movie," Becca says.

Tristan grins as he unlocks the door of the small wooden building (Becca called it a shack, but Tristan takes offense to that) at the edge of the property.

"I loved coming out here when I was a kid," Tristan says, feeling nostalgic as he steps in and flips on the light switch. Two bulbs hanging from the ceiling flood the space with light, and Tristan breathes in the comforting scent of mulch and dirt. "When I was about seven," he explains turning to Becca, "I watched this movie—I can't remember the name of it now—anyway, it was about this kid who made money mowing lawns, and I thought it was the coolest thing ever." He lets out an embarrassed laugh, because he's never told anyone about this before. "I was obsessed with mowing lawns. Of course, we always had landscapers, so I never had to do any chores like that, but I wanted to. One of the landscapers, his name was Jack. He used to tend to all the flowers in the spring and the summer, and he had a son about my age at home, so he took a liking to me.

He let me come out here when he was working and watch everything he was doing. I had to sneak out so my parents wouldn't find out about it, but my nanny at the time was in on it. She'd pack a lunch for both of us and I'd bring it out here and watch him repot plants. After we finished, he'd fire up the lawnmower and let me go to town on the grass back here. We had to be really careful so my mom wouldn't see. Had the time of my life."

"Mowing the lawn?" she asks, very softly. There's a hint of amusement in her voice and tears in her eyes, and he's immediately glad he brought her here. "I wish I would've known you as a kid. I used to mow lawns for money. I would've let you do the mowing, and I would've given you a cut of the profits."

Tristan laughs; he's so glad he brought her here. He stands by the doorway, looking at the carved lines in the frame: every summer Jack would make Tristan stand with his back against it so he could carve a line out to mark how much he'd grown.

"Is that a growth chart?" Becca asks, running her finger

over the top line. It's from when he was twelve, the last summer he was home. The following years he was sent to camp that lasted from June through August, right before school started again.

"Yeah, Jack said he did that with his son, so…"

"And your parents didn't," she replies under her breath, so quietly he's certain he wasn't supposed to hear it. She turns and faces him, then wraps her mittened hands around the lapels of his coat and pulls him down into a long, tender kiss. "What else did you miss out on?"

He thinks for a minute, replies, "Snowball fights."

"Seriously?" she asks, looking suspicious. "Because you went to boarding school, and if there's anything rich boys would do while walking across your idyllic campus courtyards, it would be a snowball fight."

Tristan steps back and out the door, Becca watching him intently all the while. Then he bends down, eyes still on hers, and grabs a handful of snow.

"Don't you dare," she says slowly. "I have great aim, and I throw really hard."

Tristan tosses the snow aside, then stands up and kisses her. "Wanna head back? I bet I can wrangle up some hot chocolate."

"Mmmm," Becca hums against his lips. "That sounds amazing."

Tristan follows her out the door, then locks it. He's just getting ready to turn and take her hand when he feels a wet sting on the back of his neck. There's a smattering of snow on his shoulder, and he can hear Becca giggling. It's a sound that makes him smile, and he can't help but laugh himself.

"What do you think you're doing?" he asks, scrambling for snow as he dodges the next snowball she throws. He has to admit that she does have great aim, and she also throws really hard, just like she said she does.

She ducks as he throws a snowball at her, but he manages to clip her shoulder just as she nails him right in the center of the chest. Her eyes are bright and her cheeks are rosy, and he doesn't think he's ever seen her look more beautiful.

"Making memories," she says. "That's what I'm doing."

Tristan grins, lets himself feel the weight of that statement for a moment before he lobs another snowball at her. It explodes on her jacket and into her hair, and she looks down in surprise and just laughs. Their fight lasts for a while, until their arms hurt and Becca is shivering. She really needs that hot chocolate. Tristan surrenders, just wanting to get her inside, but as he starts to walk away she manages to tackle him into a snowbank.

He rolls to his side, props himself up over her using his elbows, and they both smile at each other like idiots.

He thought he felt it many times before; hell, he even tried to make himself feel it.

Now, with her, he *knows*. He doesn't have to make himself feel anything, because it's there. Everywhere. All the time.

This is what falling in love feels like.

CHAPTER
Nineteen

This is a crazy plan and Becca knows it; she can feel it down deep in her bones. She's been thinking about it ever since she came back from her walk with Tristan. He shared a little bit of his childhood with her, and after she adds that to what she already knows about him, she realizes that if someone doesn't stop Clay Blackwell from packing the weight of the world on Tristan's shoulders, he's going to buckle under the pressure. She doesn't know when and she doesn't know how, but he will. Soon.

She has to confront Clay about it. Clearly nothing else has gotten through to him, and she thinks it might be good for him to hear from an outsider what an incredibly shitty father he's been to his son. He has 28 years of mistakes to make up for, and it's time he started doing that.

Becca manages to find Clay's office by following one of the

cooks from the kitchen. She's sure she looks like a complete lunatic, skulking around corners, waiting for someone to emerge. Her opportunity presents itself in the form of after-dinner coffee. Becca can smell the aroma as she follows the woman carrying the cup on a silver tray, because of course he'd want his coffee served to him on a silver tray. Of course. The woman slips into Clay's office, and unfortunately for Becca that leaves her with time to rethink her plan.

She really hopes she can have her conversation with Clay before someone comes looking for her. Tristan's in the living room talking to his mother, and Becca took the opportunity to slip away, excusing herself for a warm bath. Probably not the smartest excuse, since she's pretty sure Tristan might take that as an invitation to join her and find that she's not in his room, but there's nothing she can do about that now. She needs uninterrupted time with his father, and she's going to get it.

Again, she knows this is a terrible idea, but the man she loves is in a difficult position: he wants to do as his father wishes, but he doesn't want to live his life the way his father wants. There's no winning in that situation, and Becca wants Tristan to *win*. She wants him to have choices and not be saddled with some legacy that he might not want to be a part of. Deep down, she knows she should butt out of this, because it's none of her business. Thing is, she's falling in love with Tristan and she thinks he might be falling in love with her, too. And this, this could be their *life*. It's one that she doesn't want, and he knows he doesn't either.

He'll be upset with her if he finds out what she's doing;

she just hopes that the good outweighs the bad. Underneath all the uncertainty, she knows deep down in her gut that this is the right thing to do, and Becca's never regretted following her instincts.

She paces up and down the short corridor to the right of Clay's office, careful to stay hidden so the woman from the kitchen doesn't see her when she leaves. She's sure to tip off Tristan if that happens. She wishes the woman would hurry up and get out of there already; Becca's uncomfortable in this huge, drafty place with its ornate decorations and ridiculously large chandeliers every few feet.

Finally, when the coast is clear, Becca walks up Clay's office. She paces a few times, knowing this is the last time for her to abort this plan. No. No, she's going to do it. She wipes her sweaty palms across her hips, then raises her shaking hand to the door and knocks.

The door creaks open, and she sticks her head in, not willing to wait for an invitation.

The sound of the door makes Clay look up, and his eyes are hard and appraising as he studies Becca, standing there with her knees shaking. She wonders if there's ever a time when he doesn't have this stony, emotionless mask on. Was there a day in his life when he was blissfully happy? Even a little happy? Becca can't imagine what happiness would look like on this man.

"May I help you, Miss Smith?" He asks, his voice cold.

"You may," Becca replies, testing her voice before it really matters. It's clear and steady, thankfully. If it was shaky, he'd be able to tell she was nervous. Clay Blackwell is a shark, and she absolutely cannot let him smell blood.

"Please," he says, standing up and motioning toward the leather chair that's in front of his desk. "Have a seat."

Becca grips the back of the chair as she pulls it out, then sits down. To keep her hands from shaking, she laces her fingers together and rests them on her lap.

"I'm very busy," Clay says, looking down at the screen of his laptop. "So I'd appreciate it if you would keep it short."

"I'll keep it very short," Becca replies confidently, which gets Clay's attention. "Your son loves you, and he wants you to love him. The way you treat him is atrocious, and I want it to stop."

Not that Becca's surprised, but Clay actually has the audacity to *laugh* at her, and that just pisses her off. She's positive he's written off many people with a laugh and a sarcastic smile, but that's not going to happen here today.

"You certainly have an interesting definition of atrocious treatment," he tells her. "I'd hate to think of what you think of truly atrocious behavior."

"I don't have any children, but I know that giving and withholding money isn't parenting. I know that a trust fund isn't a substitute for a father, and that all the money in the world means nothing if the people who are supposed to love you don't support you."

"Oh, I've supported Tristan." Clay straightens his back and rests his forearms on the desk, leaning toward Becca as he speaks. "I've supported him through Ivy League colleges and half-assed attempts at learning about the business that gave him a roof over his head, put food on the table and provided him with the kind of life most people can only dream of. All he has done for most of his life is squander that support."

Becca takes a deep breath, trying to control her urge to yell. "Did you ever stop to ask him if the kind of life most people can only dream of is the kind of life he wants?"

"What he wants is to be lazy and irresponsible, so, no. I've never asked him, because what he wants is unacceptable. I demand excellence from him."

Becca sighs and shakes her head. "You demand obedience from him, and you withhold your love unless he gives it to you. That's no way to live a life. You think you're asking him to be responsible, but what you're asking him is to be like you!"

"Of course I want him to be like me!" Clay yells, pounding his fist on the desk. "I'm like my father, and my father was like this. That's the way you live the lives that we lead; that's what it means to have a legacy. In order to pass that legacy onto the next generation, they must be equipped to handle it. Do you think my own father didn't treat me the same way?"

Becca sits on the edge of her seat, desperate to get through to this stubborn, nasty man. "Don't you want things to be different for him? Don't you want him to have more than one path in life? Don't you want him to have choices?"

"I gave him all the choices he needs. Make an effort in life, get involved in a business I approve of. Show he cares about anything, or I'll disinherit him. Why do you think you're here this weekend? Don't think for a second I don't know he's trying to buy himself some time."

All the breath leaves Becca's body, and her eyes go wide before she has a chance to school her expression. She's so stunned, at this point she doesn't care that Clay can see it written all over her face.

When Becca sees the amused look Clay gives her, she realizes she does care that he knows he surprised her. "He didn't tell you I'm disinheriting him?"

"No," she answers breathily.

Clay leans back, looking like he thinks he's won this battle. "He told me he thought you were different. I guess you aren't so different after all."

"What's that supposed to mean?" Becca asks, offended.

"It means that you're just like all the other women who drape themselves all over him on those goddamn gossip sites."

"I don't care if Tristan has money or not," she replies, and that is the absolute truth.

"The look on your face told me otherwise, Miss Smith," he replies, turning back to whatever it is he was working on earlier. "And the fact that he didn't tell you tells me Tristan's not so sure about that either."

"The look on my face was surprise that he thought that about me. The look on my face was shock that he brought me here to prove something to you, because he felt like he had to. What I'm sure about is that Tristan would give you every penny he has and every dime he's set to inherit if you would treat him like a son. But me? I'd be with him either way."

Clay narrows his eyes at her. "Oh, I'm sure you would," he says condescendingly. "Do you have anything else you'd like to accuse me of? Any more parenting wisdom you'd like to impart on me?"

"Nothing that you'd listen to," Becca says bitterly.

"Good. Now if you don't mind, I need to get back to my work. My father left me an empire to run, it requires a lot of my attention."

Becca stands and gives him a long, sad look. "I'm sure it does. Keeps you from having to live your life, doesn't it? Being holed up in your office all the time, devoid of feeling. I bet you have no idea why your son doesn't want to be like you."

She walks to the door with measured steps, then shuts it behind her.

She manages to make it halfway down the hall before she starts crying.

Becca's hands are shaking as she hastily folds up what clothes she'd taken out of her suitcase. She walks into Tristan's bathroom, making sure she has everything; she doesn't ever want to come back here again. She takes a look at her watch, counting down the seconds until the cab company told her the cab she'd called for would arrive to pick her up. She still has another ten minutes; just enough time for Tristan to come looking for her and kill her resolve to leave.

She just needs some space. She needs to go back to the city and take a step back from this for a little while. She needs to think about what's going on between the two of them.

Becca had been wondering if she and Tristan were moving too fast and now she had her definitive answer: yes. Absolutely yes. After only a month they hadn't had a talk about exclusivity, even though she hadn't gone out with anyone else and she was fairly certain that Tristan hadn't either. And yet here she is, crying in his stately bedroom because he hadn't been honest with her.

It's almost crushing, knowing there's a part of him that thinks she wants him for his money, that she wouldn't want to be with him if he didn't have it. If he had told her the real reason he wanted her to visit with him, she probably would've come. She wouldn't have approved of Tristan kowtowing to his father's ridiculous demands, but she would've come anyway, just to support him.

She would've done that because she's falling in love with him. She runs her hands through her hair and looks down at her packed suitcase, feeling the tears welling up again, because part of him thought maybe she wanted him for his money, and part of her was still surprised when she woke up in the morning and he was still there with her.

Oh, what a pair they are.

Becca zips her suitcase and puts it on the floor, then pulls on the telescoping handle.

"Becca?"

He has her heart racing at just the sound of her name. Does she stand any kind of a chance with this man at all? She swipes at her face, then turns and sees him standing in the doorway. He looks shocked and more than a little panicked.

"What…" He takes a few steps forward. "What are you doing? What happened? Where are you going?"

"I need to go home," Becca says, sounding completely heartbroken.

In a few long strides he's standing right in front of her, cupping her cheek and swiping her tears away. "Why? Is everything okay."

Gently, Becca clasps his wrist and lowers it. She can't do this if he's touching her. She's not even sure she can do it if he isn't. "Why didn't you tell me your father is threatening to disinherit you?"

Maybe they've both moved too far too fast, but Becca can practically see his heart sinking. It's written all over his face. "He told you that? Did he find you just to tell you that?" The heartbreak has quickly moved to anger. She can hear it in his voice.

"No," Becca sobs, shaking her head. "I went to him. I wanted to talk to him about you."

He steps back. "Becca," he replies. "What did you say?"

CHAPTER
Twenty

*B*ecca talked to his father. Without asking him.

He's simultaneously impressed by and proud of her, but also so fucking angry he almost can't see straight. He takes deep breaths, trying to calm his nerves. He's got to rein this in; he doesn't even know what she said to him.

"What did you say to him?" he asks again, proud of how steady his voice is this time.

She shrugs, looking over at him with red-rimmed, tired eyes. "I told him to stop forcing his life on you, to pay attention to what you want and to stop using love and money as leverage so that you'll let him have his way."

"Why did you do that?" He knows he shouldn't be mad at her, but he didn't want her to find out about his inheritance this way. He definitely didn't want her talking to his father alone. Ever. What else could he have said that she isn't telling him?

Becca crosses her arms over her chest and looks at the floor. "When you took me out this afternoon and told me about how you grew up, with a *landscaper* doing things for you that your parents should've done, Tristan, I…I felt so angry at him. And that was after only knowing him a few hours! I can't imagine what it was like for you growing up with that. I wanted to let him know how shitty a father he was to you, that even I—someone who doesn't even know him—can see it. I want better for you than that."

Tristan can't believe what he's hearing, and he's struck by a wave of affection for this woman that nearly drowns him.

"So," he begins carefully. "You're not upset about the money?"

"What, the possibility of you losing it?" She looks absolutely wrecked. Of all the ways Tristan thought he would hurt her, this definitely was not one of them. "Have I ever done anything that made you think I would be?"

She doesn't look angry at him, and the question isn't accusatory. She genuinely wants to know.

"No," he whispers. "Never."

"Then why would you think-"

Tristan cuts her off, needing her to understand where he's coming from. "For as long as I could remember, my dad always told me that people would want to be around me because of the prestige that came along with our name, hoping that hanging out with me would give them the same kind of lifestyle that I had. The more my relationship with him deteriorated, the more I started falling in with some people who weren't good for me. I was determined to prove him wrong, when all I ever did was prove him right. They were hanging out with me so I could get them into a club, get them on a red carpet, or because I had my own jet.

The longer that went on, the more I figured that people didn't see much in me except dollar signs, that I wasn't worth more than my money."

"Tristan," she says sadly.

"It's not that I thought that you were one of those people, it was that the more time I spent with you, the more afraid I was that I would find out that you were. Obviously I know now that fear was completely unfounded, but...if I had found that out about you, it would've devastated me."

"I think you're worth more than anyone realizes," she says. "You're worth so much. And it's not tied to your name or your father's money or your family's legacy, Tristan."

Her phone buzzes, and she pulls it out of her pocket.

"My cab is here," she says, grabbing the handle of her suitcase.

"You called a cab?" He can't let her walk out of here alone tonight, he just can't. If she needs a ride back to the city, he'll take her.

"I told you, I need to go home."

"I'll take you home," he says, reaching for her suitcase. "A cab will cost an arm and a leg."

"You're not taking me home." He recognizes the steely glint in her eye and the firm set of her jaw. He can argue with her about this all he wants, but he's not going to win. "I need to take a step away, Tristan. This is moving too fast. I knew it was, but I wanted…"

"What did you want?" he asks, feeling the crackling electricity between them. Even when they're angry and heartbroken and one of her fingers is barely touching his as they both grip the handle of her suitcase, he can feel the connection between them.

"I wanted this to be real," she says, choking on a sob at the end as she walks way, rolling her bag behind her.

He follows her. How could he not?

"This *is* real," he tells her as she quickly makes her way to the front door.

"How real can it be, Tristan? You were afraid I was here for your money, and I wake up every other morning surprised that you haven't run out in the middle of the night."

She starts putting her coat on, and he just stands there, stunned. That one hurt, but he can't deny that he deserves it. "Becca," he says softly. "I'm not going anywhere."

Once she has her coat on, she turns to him. She's biting her lip, and he can tell she's trying like hell not to cry. "We went too fast, Tristan. We went from a one night stand that never happened to *this*. We need to take a step back and just figure things out."

"What's there to figure out?" he asks. If there was ever a time to lay it all on the line, it's now. If she's going to walk alway from him, she's going to walk away from him knowing exactly how he feels about her.

"We aren't ready for this."

"I'm ready," he tells her. "I'm ready for this. Becca, I'm falling in love with you."

"How do you know?"

"I know it. I *feel* it. Don't leave. Let me prove to you that I'm not going anywhere."

She's looking down, and he steps closer, thankful when she doesn't move away. He cups her face in his hands, leans down and kisses her, but all too soon she pulls away.

"I have to go," she whispers. "I need some space."

"Is this it then? The end of me and you?"

She swallows, and it's an eternity until she says, "No."

If he has to, he can deal with that answer. "Okay," he replies reluctantly. "Let me walk you out."

He follows her out the front door and down the steps. He watches as the cabbie opens the door for her and she slips inside, very pointedly looking down at her hands, which are clasped in her lap. He wonders if she thinks that looking at him will make her want to stay.

He starts to call out her name, but then he realizes that if he cares about her—if he's *falling in love with her* like he knows he is—then he'll give her the space that she wants. So, he walks over to the cabbie and hands him all the cash in his wallet.

"This should cover the trip and a nice tip for you," he says.

The cabbie nods and gets in the car.

Protective as ever, Tristan takes note of the license plate number and the cab company as it rounds the circled driveway. He pulls out his phone and types out a text to Becca. "Please let me know when you get home, okay?"

The second he hits send, he hears the shrill sound of rubber screeching against asphalt and the sickening crunch of metal.

CHAPTER
Twenty-One

*B*ecca can hear someone calling her name, but it's distant, like an echo. Too far away.

She tries to open her eyes using all her might, but she can only see blurs. There's too much light and so much fuzziness. Her heart is racing, beating in time to the steady throbbing that's reaching its long, painful fingers across every single part of her body. The only relief from the panic comes when she hears Tristan calling her name.

He's worried, she can tell by the way his voice is trembling, but he's trying to keep her calm.

"It's okay," he says. "It's gonna be okay."

There's frantic yelling in the background, but Becca can't make any of it out. She just focuses on Tristan's voice and the steady slide of his hand along the top of her head. It distracts her from the pain.

She tries to say his name, but it just comes out in a painful, scratchy rasp.

"Shhh," he says, his lips close to her ear. She can feel them. "Don't talk, okay? I'm here, it's going to be all right."

She reaches for his hand, wanting something to hold onto and God, the *pain*.

"Don't move, Becca. Please," he says, crying. "Help is coming, everything is going to be okay. Just stay with me, okay? Stay with me."

CHAPTER
Twenty-Two

Tristan's had the good fortune in his life of never having to spend any time in a hospital. This particular one, not too far from his parents' home, has an excellent reputation but is more cold and sterile than Tristan was expecting. He thinks that people desperate for news on their injured and ill loved ones should have more than uncomfortable furniture to sit on and stale coffee to drink while they wait.

So Tristan doesn't sit, and he doesn't drink the terrible coffee. He paces back and forth on the far side of the waiting room, that's blessedly empty apart from him and his mother, who is sitting in the corner thumbing through a magazine. She looks up at him every minute or so, and he expects her to tell him to sit down because he's going wear a hole in the carpet, but she doesn't.

Abby and Cole are on their way to the hospital from the

city. Becca's mom is on a flight that's still too damn far away as her daughter's being prepped for surgery.

What's he supposed to do? Sit idle in the hospital after Becca was in an accident that he really can't help blaming himself for?

Logically, he knows it's not his fault. He wasn't the driver who lost control on the ice and broadsided the cab Becca rode in, but he was the reason she was in the cab in the first place. He should've been honest with her. He should've insisted that they sit down and talk through their issues like the adults that they are. He knew she was still leery of his ability to stick around, and it would've given him a chance to broach the subject of money. He realizes now of course that they were going too fast, that they were moving along trying to gloss over their issues, hoping to cover them up enough so that they wouldn't come up again.

He was right about one thing, though: he is goddamn terrible at relationships. Surprisingly, this failure and their fight aren't setbacks for him. If anything, they convince him that he wants to work through their issues. He wants to *fight* for her. All she has to do is come out of the operating room alive, and they can handle the rest together.

As Tristan walks past the television, he turns the volume up a little higher, hoping the sound of the anchor reading the news will distract him enough that he'll stop thinking about the accident. The sickening sound of the crash, the way his lungs burned when he ran down the driveway, and the feeling of his heart cracking in two when he saw what had happened. He plops down in the chair next to his mother, fights against the memory of the huge gash near Becca's hairline, her blood dripping down her forehead, the twisted angle her left leg was bent into, and the wheezing sound that rattled her chest when she breathed.

Tristan flinches when he feels his mother's hand on his back.

"It's going to be okay," she says. "Becca's going to be okay." She punctuates the sentiment by leaning forward and pressing her lips against his cheek.

Tristan swallows against the painful lump in his throat. "We had a fight," he says, his voice wavering. "We had a fight, and I let her leave."

"I know, sweetheart." The comforting circuit she rubs along his spine makes his heartbeat come close to returning to normal. "It's not your fault."

"I should've told her about Dad," he says, looking at his mother through watery eyes. "She wouldn't have cared. I was worried she would, but that was stupid of me. She would've come if I had asked her to; she doesn't care about the money."

His mother nods. "I realized that when I overheard you two talking the other day. Before your walk."

There's something about hearing his mother confirm it that settles his nerves. "She told dad off," he says with a wet laugh, then turns and catches the grin on his mother's face.

"I know that, too." She takes his hand in hers and squeezes tight. "You need to hold onto this one."

Tristan nods. "I know."

In the small hours of the morning, Tristan's mom dozes in the same chair she's been sitting in all night, her head propped up against the wall.

Abby and Cole are holding hands in the chairs directly across from him. Abby's eyes are red-rimmed and bloodshot from crying, and she's resting her head on Cole's shoulder. She and Becca's mom, Michelle, had been talking, but Michelle easily slipped into motherly mode, insisting that Abby get some sleep. Now, she's sitting next to Tristan, and Cole keeps looking at him with pity in his eyes, and it's too goddamn much.

Michelle Smith is a tiny, blonde breath of fresh air, even in her grief. She's soft-spoken and comforting, and just what the people who love Becca need. Even though they should be the ones comforting her, she doesn't rest long enough for them to say the words. Maybe she's afraid of hearing them, Tristan doesn't know.

"I'm sorry we had to meet like this," Tristan says, unable to come up with anything other than a simple apology that he's already offered her a dozen times since she arrived.

"Me too," she says with a sad smile. "I knew when my girl visited at Thanksgiving that she had met someone before she even told me about you. Then, of course, when she did tell me about you, her whole face lit up." Michelle smiles at him, and she looks so much like Becca it hurts.

"I care about your daughter a lot," he replies. He should

probably tell Michelle that "care" is a lot closer to "love," but he thinks that's something that Becca should hear from him first. "We fought tonight, I-"

"Oh, hush," Michelle says, taking his hand between her tiny ones. "I know my daughter. She's a headstrong woman, and once she's got her mind set on something, there isn't a damn thing that's going to stop her. As for why she got in the cab, well…she doesn't have the best track record with some people sticking around. She's been a bit skittish when it comes to love since she was a kid. It's not your fault."

Tristan takes a deep breath. "It's a little bit my fault. She might've had some issues, but I didn't do anything to help them."

"You will," she says. "When she gets out, you will."

He nods. "Yeah," he tells her. "I will."

Michelle looks at him like she's got all the faith in the world in him, and he begins to understand how this woman could make Becca feel like everything was right in the world even when she was struggling. She's doing it for Tristan now, and he's a complete stranger to her.

"It's going to be okay," he tells her, his voice steady and sure. "She's going to be okay."

Michelle's eyes well up, but she presses her lips together and nods. "I can't lose my girl," she says, squeezing his hand.

Tristan squeezes back. She's going to be okay, there is no other option.

When the doctor comes out half an hour later with a hopeful smile and good news, they all truly breathe for the first time in hours.

Becca has suffered a pierced lung, three broken ribs, a concussion, countless scrapes and bruises, and a broken leg, but she's going to be okay with some rest and recovery and a little bit of physical therapy. Honestly, it's about the best Tristan could've hoped for when he saw Becca immediately after the accident.

She's recovering from surgery now, and after, she'll be moved to the intensive care unit.

Becca's mother is grinning from ear to ear, the doctor's news buoying her spirits. She hugged and kissed Abby and Cole and shooed them off to rest for the night. Tristan's mother has gone home, but Tristan doesn't want to leave Michelle here alone. She, however, isn't having any of that.

"Go on now," she says. "Go home and get some rest. I spoke to one of the nurses, and the hospital has a closed ICU policy; I'm not sure if we'll be able to convince someone to let you visit while Beck's in there." She must see Tristan's face fall, because she follows it up with a quick, "But I'm gonna try."

He just wants to hold Becca's hand, to press his lips against her warm skin. He wants to hear the steady beat of her heart and know that she's not going anywhere, but he doesn't want to whine about it. Becca needs her mother, that's the most important thing, and he's not going to make this more difficult for her by complaining about a visitation policy that neither one of them have any control over.

"Do you need anything?" Tristan asks. "I can bring you some food or a change of clothes. I'll have one of our spare rooms made up so you have a place to stay if you need it, although I'm sure you'll want to stay here as much as you can."

Michelle smiles warmly at him. "Abby and Cole have offered me a room at their house if I need it, but…give me your phone number and I'll call you if I need anything. I'll call you if anything happens."

"I'm not going to be gone long," he assures her before he watches her program his number into her cellphone.

She gives him a warm hug and says, "I know you won't."

Back at his parents' house, in the shower, Tristan scrubs his arms until the skin is raw and red, trying to get the remnants of Becca's blood off his skin, from where it crept up under the cuff of his shirt. He hadn't even noticed it was there, and it takes forever for him to feel clean again.

After he's dried and dressed, he wanders out to his room and lowers himself onto his bed. He could've kept going for as long as he needed to, but now that he's home and he knows Becca's okay and he's got a moment to think, the fatigue sets in. He's weary, down to his bones. He rests his head on his pillow, then grabs the pillow Becca used and lays his head on it. It still smells like her shampoo, and he breathes deep.

He almost lost her today, and the reality of it is too much

to take.

When Becca wakes up, he promises himself that he's not going to waste another second with her.

He's not going to fuck this up again.

CHAPTER
Twenty-Three

$\mathcal{B}$ecca's slowly pulled out of sleep by a pounding ache that touches every single centimeter of her body, inside and out. Her head is throbbing, and there's an incessant beeping that she can't figure out the source of. Breathing hurts. *Existing* hurts. Her limbs feel like anvils, impossible to move. She can feel that there's a hand holding hers; the warmth of it is nice to feel, and the hand is soft like her mother's. Is her mother here?

She turns her head what little bit she can, and she's instantly sorry she did. It takes every ounce of effort she has to open her eyes, and even the dim light is too much. She groans—at least she thinks she does—in annoyance, and the hand that is holding hers tightens its grip.

"Beck?"

It *is* her mom. She can make out the vague outline of her,

but just the sound of her voice is nice. But what's she doing here? What happened that resulted in her mom being here, holding her hand? The annoying beeping in the background speeds up.

There's a hand in her hair, smoothing it down, and that calms her immediately. Even though she's not sure what happened or what's going on, the comforting gesture from her childhood is enough to soothe Becca.

"Shhhh," her mother says. "It's okay."

"Happ'nd?" Becca manages. Her throat feels raw and shredded, like she swallowed a thousand knives.

"You were in an accident, baby. You're a little banged up, but you're going to be okay."

Becca reaches far back into the broken-up shards of memories that are scattered in her brain. The last thing she remembers is sirens and pain and Tristan trying to hold it together while he begged her to calm down. Oh god, they'd had a fight…

"Mom?" It's easier to talk this time, even though it still hurts like hell.

"Yeah?" she says, still running her fingers through Becca's hair.

"How long?" she asks, hoping her mother will understand what she's getting at.

Thankfully, she does. "Three days."

God, Becca thinks. Three days of her life gone, just like that.

"Abby's out in the waiting room, and Tristan…"

There goes that damned beeping again, but this time it

makes her mother smile.

"We snuck him in a few times to see you. You have a friendly night nurse who thinks he's charming. But they're going to move you later, and he and Abby will be able to spend all the time with you they want, okay? But you need to rest, sweetheart. Can you do that for me?"

Becca nods tiredly. Rest sounds good. She hears a click and feels an almost immediate rush of calm flood through her body, and the pain blessedly stops.

"Just sleep," she says in that voice she used to use when Becca was small and had a nightmare. "I'll be here when you wake up."

It's nice, knowing her mother will be here when she wakes up, and she hears Tristan's name somewhere way off in the distance as the heavy hand of sleep pulls her under.

CHAPTER
Twenty-Four

$\mathcal{B}$ecca is in the ICU for three long days, during which Michelle manages to sneak him back with the aid of the friendly night nurse a handful of times. Becca's sleeping, resting, but just sitting close to her and holding her hand is enough to get him through. If he's completely honest, being near to her like this, seeing first hand the damage that was done to her, it scares the shit out of him. It hammers home how delicate life is and how easily he could've lost her. It makes keeping secrets over something so inconsequential as money seem incredibly stupid, and all he can do is sit there and think about it.

Becca's moved out of ICU on Wednesday afternoon, and he cannot describe the utter joy he feels when he walks in and sees her with a little more color in her cheeks and fewer tubes running in and out of her. She still has quite a few bruises that are angry blues and purples and yellows, and her leg is still in a cast, but she's alive and breathing on her own and it's the most beautiful sight in the world.

Tristan, Abby and Michelle take turns sitting with her, so she's rarely ever alone. They read to her and talk to her. Sometimes they sleep while she sleeps because exhaustion is setting in, but they all try like hell not to let it show.

On Thursday, Tristan walks into Becca's room with two bags in his hands, and sits down in the hard, uncomfortable chair next to her bed. Thankfully she's still sleeping.

"She didn't get much rest last night," Becca's nurse whispers to him. "We had quite the morning."

Tristan knew this, Michelle texted him as much. In fact, she asked him to come early because she needed to take a break; she was worried that the two of them were headed for an epic argument, and this is not the time or place.

So, Tristan brought something to distract her from going stir crazy, but he's glad she's resting. He's happy to sit here and wait for her to wake up.

He leans back in his chair and slides down, letting his legs stretch out in front of him. The low, rhythmic noises of the hospital are almost enough to lull him to sleep. He turns his head, catches sight of her IV pump. He's looked at this thing countless times over the past few days, but today, something catches his eye. In the bottom right hand corner is a familiar emblem. Underneath it, a familiar name.

Blackwell Technologies.

He sits up, eyes wide. He's floored. Obviously he knows a lot about the front office of his family's company, but his father has always been a big picture guy. Blackwell Technologies is a conglomerate that dabbles in all areas of tech, but Tristan had no idea they had anything to do with medical devices.

Yet here his name is on a machine that's keeping Becca out of pain. He wonders how many other machines his name is on in this hospital and others, keeping people alive. It's a watershed moment for him, one where the fog clears and he thinks about something other than bottom lines and investor relations and stock prices.

His family's company does good in this world.

"Hey," Becca says sleepily. Her eyes are half-lidded as she looks over at him, a small smile playing at her lips. Tristan sits up and gives her a soft kiss, grinning when she hums against him.

"How do you feel?" he asks as he slides his hand through her hair.

"Like I got hit by a car," she answers.

"Not funny."

"I'm better now," she replies, making his heart skip a beat. "I want out of here."

"I know," Tristan says, taking her hand. "Your doctor says you can probably go home on Sunday."

She pouts, and even though Tristan knows it's not supposed to be cute, it is. "Christmas is on Friday."

"I know." He slides the pad of his thumb along her temple. "But your mom and I will be here, and so will Abby and Cole. We're trying to talk the nurses into letting us bring you some dinner. I'm going to try to talk your night nurse into it; the one you have now is a tough nut to crack."

"You have better things to do than spend Christmas here, Tristan," she says, turning away from him.

Gently, he presses his hand against her cheek and turns her head so she's looking at him. Now's as good a time as any for this talk.

"I want to be where you are, Becca."

She sighs and presses her lips together. He knows he's about to be on the receiving end of an out, but he's not going to take it. Not with her, not ever.

He takes her hand in his and threads their fingers together, resting his other arm on the bed so he can lean in close to her.

"We left things in a bad place-"

"We don't have to talk about this now."

"I do," Tristan says firmly. "I need to say this, okay? Because I almost lost you, and if that had happened and I hadn't said this…"

"Okay," Becca whispers, wide awake now. "Okay."

"The other night you said that we were moving too fast. We're not moving too fast for me, but I think part of the problem is that I never sat down with you and told you what my intentions are with you. That was because of my own insecurities, Becca. The very first thing I should've done after the way I treated you when we first met is to let you know what I wanted with you. It hurt me when you told me the other night that you were still surprised sometimes when you woke up and I was still there, but I deserved that. Leaving you the way I did that night at the beach was one of the biggest regrets of my life, but at the same time I'm glad I did it," he says, squeezing her hand. "It got me to the point where I was ready to be with you. I'm sorry that I let my insecurities keep me from telling you about the money. You've never done anything to make me think that my bank account is why you're with me. In fact, the opposite. I used to offer up my jet to women to impress them; you're the first one who's ever turned it down."

Tristan dares too look up and is happy to see that Becca's still listening. She's a little teary, but the small smile on her face balances it out. She reaches up and places her hand on his cheek, and Tristan leans into it, glad for the warm, familiar feeling.

"Well, the fact that you have a chef is nice, I can't deny that."

Tristan laughs. Here she is, in a *hospital bed*, and she's trying to lighten the mood. He leans in and gives her a kiss.

"I want us to be together. Exclusive. No one else. And I promise I will be there every morning when you wake up for as long as you want me to be. You said you needed space, and I'll give you all the space you need. I know you were angry with me and you probably still are, and I don't blame you for that. But after what happened…I just had to tell you how I feel."

"Yeah?"

"Yeah. It's been a month and I know it's fast, but I've never felt like this about anyone before. I love you, I *know* it. I can wait for you to get there. Just…for now, I want to be with you. I want you to want to be with me."

Becca grins at him. "I want to be with you."

"I know I don't have the best track record, but…wait, did you say you want to be with me?" That kind of takes away the sting of her not returning his 'I love you.'

"Yes," she laughs. "I did say that. I have a condition though."

Tristan nods, fairly certain that he'll agree to anything at this point. "Okay."

"I want you to end this fight you're having with your father."

"Becca," he sighs.

"I let you talk, now you let me, okay?"

"Okay."

She takes a breath. "This thing between you and your dad, it's making you miserable. If you and I are going to have any kind of life together, I don't want that misery to be a part of it. I want you to be happy. If he has some break-your-back conditions under which he won't cut you off and you don't want to or can't meet those conditions, then don't. It's not worth your happiness, Tristan. But if your relationship with him is important, and you don't think you'll be able to deal with him not being in your life, and you want to make things right, then do that, okay? At least try."

"I can do that," he says softly.

"Promise me."

Tristan indulges her. "I promise."

"You need to make peace with some stuff, and so do I. I know that. So you work on your stuff, and I'll work on mine and we'll see if we can make this work together, okay?"

He nods, then kisses her. "Sounds like a plan."

When he pulls away, Becca's eyes are bright. "What's in the bags?"

Tristan smiles and kisses her again. He reaches in one bag and pulls out her tablet. She practically squeals when she takes it from him.

"I put some of your favorite movies on there so you'd have something to watch."

"Thank you!"

"I brought your favorite pajamas, your slippers, and some other stuff."

"What other stuff?"

Tristan pulls the tray by her table further up so he can stack things on it. He pulls out a few packs of construction paper, two pairs of scissors, glue, glitter, markers and tape.

"What's this?" she asks, even though he knows that she knows the answer.

"We're gonna make a Christmas tree." He slides a pen and some scissors over to Becca as he rips open the packet of green paper. "Your mom and Abby are going to help you with the ornaments. You and I are going to make the tree. When you start feeling tired, let me know. I'll finish the rest."

She's just staring at him, and her eyes are glassy, like tears are going to spill over any second. "You remembered."

He gives her a gentle smile. "Of course I did."

Becca manages to get a good portion of the tree cut out

before she falls asleep. Tristan finishes up the rest of it and gets it taped on the wall right next to her bed without waking her up. He decides to go down and get some of the malted milk balls from the cafeteria that she likes so much. When he gets down there and grabs a bag, he spots Abby standing in line, holding a bag of the same candy.

He puts the bag down and walks over to her. "Your best friend is cheating on you, and I've gotta say that you're taking it in stride."

Abby shrugs and offers him a smile. "My balls are better, but I'm going to blame her deadened tastebuds on the terrible hospital food she's being forced to eat here. Once she gets out and goes home, everything will be back to normal."

"I'm sure that's it," he says. "I got the tree put up, you're on ornament duty."

"Oh," she replies with a smile. "Good. I bet that made her happy. That was a great idea. You off duty now?"

"I was going to buy her some candy, but you beat me to it."

Abby reaches up and pats his chest, pride brightening her eyes. "Look at you being a good boyfriend."

Tristan tries to fight it, but he blushes anyway. "I wanted to ask you about something, but I'm not sure how to do it without sounding like…well, like a privileged asshole."

Abby raises her eyebrows. "Curiosity piqued."

"I wanted to mention this to you first, because I'm not sure how all this works…I know Michelle has a job, can… can she just leave? Is she getting paid? I was worried that she might have some trouble if she missed a check or two. Same with Becca. Does she have to worry about her job, or-"

Abby stands on her tiptoes and wraps Tristan in a warm, tight hug. "Tristan," she says, grinning. "I love you so much. You are so sweet and so incredibly ignorant about the ways of the working world."

Tristan can't help but laugh, because she's right about that.

"Michelle is on family leave until just after New Year's, and she's not getting paid. Becca's on sick leave and she *is* getting paid. And the driver of the car that hit her will be reimbursing her for all the time she's lost, believe me."

Good, that's good. "I'd like to…I mean, I want to make sure that Michelle is settled." How can he tell Abby that he wants to give her money without outright saying he wants to give her money? "But I'm not sure how to broach the subject without offending her. I don't know if she has savings, or… but she shouldn't have to use any of that for this."

Abby smiles at him fondly. "That's already been taken care of."

Tristan furrows his brows, confused. "What do you mean?"

"It's already been taken care of. Michelle's pay, Becca's hospital bill. All of it. Don't tell Becca though; she doesn't know, and I don't want her getting all riled up about it when it's not necessary."

Tristan absorbs that. Who would've done it? "Did you and Cole make some arrangements?" he asks, feeling incredibly stupid that he hasn't thought of this before, but he'd been so preoccupied about Becca.

"Not me and Cole," she says, laying her hand on his forearm.

"Then who?"

She grins and says, "Your dad."

CHAPTER
Twenty-Five

"Tristan did a good job with the tree," Michelle says, surveying his handiwork. "It's only a little crooked."

Okay. It's a lot crooked, but Becca doesn't have it in her to laugh at him. "Be nice," she says, grinning. "This is his first time, he doesn't have years of practice at it like we do."

"This is true," Michelle replies as she picks up a piece of purple construction paper. "Abby, be careful with that glitter." She points at a pile Abby's using to decorate her construction paper ornament that's dangerously close to falling on the floor. "Don't give the janitors more to clean up than they have to."

"I'm sure glitter would be a nice change from bodily fluids," Becca says.

Michelle leans back in her chair and looks between Abby and Becca. "So, Christmas. We're gonna bring dinner here and hang out all day. We'll save the presents for when we get you home, how's that sound?"

"Sounds good," Becca replies as she cuts. "I don't care about presents, I just want you all here with me."

"We need to smuggle in some macaroni and cheese," Abby says.

"Mmmm," Becca moans, reaching for the silver glitter. "With the tomatoes and the-"

"Crusty stuff on top? God...yeah, we need that." Abby puts her ornament down, and she and Becca look expectantly at Michelle.

"Please make it, Mom?" Becca bats her eyelashes like she did when she was a kid.

Abby joins in with the high-pitched 'pleases' and Becca can practically see Michelle's resolve melting. This is the way they used to work her when they were younger. They were a dangerous pair, she and Abby.

"All right, all right," Michelle says, finally giving in. "Oh, it's been too long since I've had both of my girls in the same room with me." Michelle reaches out and takes Becca and Abby's hands in hers. "I miss you two all the time."

"I'm going to come for a visit soon," Abby promises.

"I'm so proud of you," Michelle says, leaning in and kissing Abby's cheek. "You finally have your own shop. And you." Michelle looks at her daughter with tears in her eyes, and Becca feels an overwhelming urge to smother her mother in hugs and kisses. Damned IVs and broken leg! "Moving up at the ad agency, just like you wanted. I need to make time to come out and see you more, see both of you enjoy the lives you've made yourselves. Next time I see you guys I don't want it to be in a hospital. I'd prefer it to be for good things."

"Yeah," Becca replies. "I would've preferred it if I hadn't gotten busted up in the back of a cab, too."

They all laugh the kind of laugh you can only let out when you know that something terrible is going to work out okay.

"So, can we talk about the reason why you were in the back of that cab?" Abby asks.

Thinking back to the conversation she had with Tristan earlier, she smiles. "I don't think that reason exists anymore."

"Oh?" Michelle asks, grinning.

"Yeah, we had a talk. I had been worrying about something that wasn't entirely Tristan's fault." She glances to her right and sees Abby's discerning eye. "Well, it was partly his fault."

"What's that?" her mother asks.

Becca shrugs. "It was about me worrying that he was going to take off," she says, pretending to be thoroughly interested in the pattern of glue she's squeezing on the construction paper circle in front of her.

"Is this about the beach?" Abby asks. "After my wedding?"

"A little, but this is about me and Dad, I think. Not feeling like I'm good enough to stick around for, and being afraid to accept that the good things in my life are going to stay good."

"Becca," Michelle says, squeezing her daughter's hand. "I had doubts about your father that I ignored for an incredibly long time. In retrospect, I knew it wasn't going to work out even before I married him. I always found ways to explain away my worries. I wasn't surprised when he took off. I was glad for myself, but sad for you. I wanted you to have a father, but he wasn't interested in being one to you, and that's his loss, baby. Not yours. Don't ever let anything that man did stop you from being happy, okay?"

Becca lets the tears that have been threatening to fall trail down her cheeks. "Okay. He actually told me that he was glad he screwed things up with me the first time, because it got him to a place where he was ready to try."

"That's the kind of thing I like to hear a man say," Michelle replies, laughing.

"I knew he would come around eventually." Abby picks up a piece of red construction paper and starts cutting another ornament.

"You don't get to say I told you so when your best friend is laid up in a hospital bed, Abs," Becca teases.

She blows Becca off. "So, you're gonna give it a shot?"

Becca nods. "Yeah. I kind of think I'm falling in love with him."

Abby just grins.

"So," Becca begins. "What's the plan for when I go home? Do I need to find a nurse, or…"

"I'll be here until a few days after New Year's," Michelle says sadly, but then I have to go home as long as you're settled. "After that, Tristan's taking over. Hopefully by then you'll be used to your crutches."

"Tristan and I are going to take turns making sure you get to your physical therapy appointments," Abby chimes in. "Tristan said he'd cook, but I'm pretty sure that was a joke.

So, his chef's services it is."

"Ugh, he makes the most amazing omelets." Becca's mouth waters just thinking about them. "The chef, not Tristan. I'm going to get used to them, and then I'm going to have to learn how to live without them."

"Maybe you won't have to," Abby says with a wink.

Michelle slaps her hand, but smiles as she picks up her pair of scissors.

Maybe, Becca thinks, trying like hell not to hope.

She hopes anyway.

CHAPTER
Twenty-Six

Tristan spends his first Christmas with Becca in a hospital room filled with her closest friends and family. There's a lopsided construction paper tree hanging on the wall, and enough (delicious) macaroni and cheese to feed an army. There aren't enough chairs for everyone to sit, so he and Cole stand, balancing paper plates in their hands. Tristan's mom stops by for a while and brings everyone cookies, and Becca eats them sitting up in bed with an obnoxious red and green ribbon tied in her hair.

It's nothing he could've ever imagined and everything he never knew he needed.

It's the first time in his life that he feels like he belongs to a *real* family.

Clay Blackwell works the day after Christmas, because, well, of course he does.

Tristan's sitting in his office, right across from him, without an ounce of nervousness in him. He's calm, he's collected, and he knows exactly what he's going to say.

To Clay's credit, he looks like he's actually interested in what that is.

"Dad," Tristan begins, lacing his fingers together as he leans forward, resting them on the desk. "I wanted to start out by thanking you for what you did for Becca and her mother."

Tristan actually hears his father's intake of breath, thinks that maybe this is the first time that he's genuinely surprised him in a way that won't require him to make a trip down to the local police station.

"Abby told me. Maybe she shouldn't have, and I don't want you to be upset with her. I asked her about it because I wanted to make sure they were both taken care of, but I wasn't sure how I could mention it without sounding trite or nosy. Or…well, like a rich asshole. You've always been better at that than I have."

"Sounding like a rich asshole?" Clay says, nearly cracking a smile.

Is his father actually joking with him? For a second Tristan wonders if he exited Connecticut and entered into an alternate dimension or something.

"No," Tristan replies, laughing. "Having tact. Anyway, it means a lot to me that you offered to do it without me asking."

Clay nods. "You're welcome."

Tristan takes a deep breath, looks his father square in his eyes. "Dad, I've spent a big chunk of my life trying to please you, even though I know you don't see it that way. I put everything I ever wanted on the back burner to focus on what you wanted me to do, what I needed to do to make you happy. Honestly, if I had my way, I never would've majored in business. I wouldn't have chosen to go to Yale. I knew that's what you wanted for me though, so that's what I did.

"I'm not going to pretend like I've always gone about things in a mature way. I fucked up, Dad, I know I have. And when I acted out at you, I hurt myself. I'm not going to take your place in the company, and it's not because I want to embarrass you, and it's not because I don't value the hard work you do or the legacy that you and grandfather built. I think that this company and the people who work for it deserve someone who is fully invested, someone whose heart is in it. Mine isn't. If admitting to that is something that gets me disinherited, then I'm okay with it. I'm not going to make myself unhappy in order to follow your dreams."

Clay doesn't interrupt, he doesn't pretend like there's something more interesting or more pressing for him to do. He just sits there quietly and listens to his son talk, probably for the first time in his life.

"That said, I know I've been aimless. I can't blame you for that, it's a result of my own stupid choices. But, I like my clubs, and I'm going to continue with the expansion that I've been working on. I'm good at managing them, and I'm successful at it. I know you think it's a frivolous investment, but it's *my* investment. I don't want to make a career out of that, though, and that's why I'm here today."

"Is that so?" Clay says, eyebrow raised. He's not being flip or condescending, which throws Tristan for a loop.

He regains his composure relatively quickly and continues on.

"When I was sitting in the hospital with Becca, I saw our name on one of the machines. I never knew we manufactured medical equipment. In all the meetings I sat in, you talked about investor relations and stock prices, but you never once mentioned anything that we did. Just seeing our emblem on that one machine got me more interested in the inner workings of this company than all the meetings I ever sat in with you. Knowing we did that? That something we develop helps save lives? I want to be a part of that, however I can. I don't know if there's an internship or some kind of apprenticeship I can take, but I'd like to do that. If being CEO of this company is something that I do at some point down the line, I want it to be something that I've earned, not something that was handed to me because my name is on the building.

"So, I'd like to get started with that, if you agree. I want to do it whether you cut me off or not. I want to be a part of this company, just…not in the way that you want me to."

Clay stands and walks to the window that overlooks their expansive, snow-covered backyard, his back turned to his son.

"Tristan, I'm not going to cut you off," he says, before turning around.

That is an answer that Tristan absolutely did not expect. "What?"

His father cracks a smile before he sits back down in his chair. "I don't think I would've ever been brave enough to tell my father to disinherit me," he says, smiling.

Leave it to his father to be proud of him for something like that. Tristan's not complaining though.

"I wanted to join the Navy. I loved airplanes back then, and I wanted to learn to fly. My father forbade it, told me that if I did something stupid and crashed—those were his actual words—that there wouldn't be anyone to run the company, and our family would be destitute. He didn't trust anyone without our name to run the company, and I let him talk me out of my dreams. When Becca came in here the other night, she gave me something to think about, and I realized that I'd been talking you out of your dreams. I don't want to do that anymore.

"I stopped by the hospital a few days ago," Clay says, giving his son a meaningful look. "I wanted to check on Becca. I know you think I'm a heartless bastard, and maybe I am, but I felt tremendous guilt over her accident, and I wanted to see how she was doing. When I arrived at her room, I saw you there. You were both sleeping. You were all hunched over the side of her bed, holding her hand." Clay gave his son a gentle smile. "It shocked the hell out of me, seeing you like that. I started to believe that maybe you were making a change, that maybe she's good for you. I think I'm right about that."

Tristan can't help but laugh, it's like a lifetime of weight has finally been lifted off his shoulders. "You are right about that, Dad. She's it for me, I know it."

The corner of Clay's mouth lifts into a wry smile. "I felt the same way about your mother."

"She makes me want to be a better man. She makes me want to leave some good in this world."

Clay nods, and for the first time in his life he gets the sense that his father actually understands him.

"So, you'll set something up?"

"Absolutely. After the new year, we'll set up a few meetings, see what you might be interested in. How's that sound?"

"It sounds really good," Tristan replies with a smile.

Clay glances at his watch. "I've got a meeting in five minutes."

Tristan nods. It's comforting to see his father behave at least a little normally. After all, Rome wasn't built in a day. He stands and shakes his father's hand.

It's a start.

Becca's mother leaves to go back to Ohio a few days into the new year. Tristan takes her to the airport. Becca argues because she wants to go, too, but he and Michelle manage to talk her out of it. Tristan doesn't mind doing it at all; he's grown really fond of Becca's mother.

"I stocked the fridge and put a few casseroles in the freezer. I know Becca likes that fancy chef you've got coming over, but sometimes you just need Mom's cooking. I left some index cards with some of her favorite recipes on them behind the coffee pot, in case she gets a hankering for anything after it's gone. You can have your chef make it, or try your hand at it yourself," she says, playfully poking him in the chest as they stand outside his car in front of the terminal. "I left some of the snacks she likes in the pantry, and went to her office and picked up some of her files. I know she doesn't want to miss any more time than she has to and they're being really good about letting her work from home so she doesn't use up more of her leave, but if she has to go in, you make sure you take her yourself, okay? None of that riding the train nonsense."

"Of course I'll take her myself," he promises, smiling at her. Some asshole cabbie is incessantly honking at him, wanting him to move, but Tristan doesn't give a shit.

"There's a list of her appointments on the fridge."

Tristan holds up his phone. "I've already put them on my calendar. I'll make sure she's there on time."

"And you better-"

"Take her myself, none of that riding the train nonsense, got it. I'll take good care of her."

Michelle smiles at him. "I know you will."

"Beck's got all of her medications and dosages and whatnot, but I left a list of those on the fridge too. Get them refilled before they run out so she's not in pain."

"I promise. You don't have to worry about anything."

Michelle leans up and wraps her arms around his neck, squeezing him tightly before she smacks a kiss on his cheek. "You take care of my girl, okay? Don't make me fly back here and kick your ass."

Tristan fights a grin, because he knows she's teasing, but…totally serious. "Believe me when I tell you that I don't want that. Also believe that I'm taking care of her because I love her, not under the threat of ass kicking."

"I know. I know she's safe with you."

Tristan's never heard another compliment that sounded so sweet. "I'll keep you updated, and I'll make sure she calls you after all of her doctor's appointments."

Michelle's given him all the instructions she can, but now it's time for her to leave, and that must be the hardest part. He can tell she's on the verge of breaking down, so he pulls her back into a hug. "I'll see you next month, right?"

She leans back and smooths her hands over his lapel. "You really don't have to fly me back here, you know."

"Yes I do," Tristan replies. "She'll be missing you by then, and she'll definitely be going stir crazy. It'll be a good surprise for her, and I'll call you about planning, I don't know… a spa day or something fun. I'll talk to Abby about it too."

"That sounds good."

Michelle pulls up the handle on her suitcase, gives him a peck on the cheek, and walks away. She turns halfway down the sidewalk and yells, "When Becca calls and lets me know how things are going, I want to know how things are going for you, too, okay?"

Tristan nods. "Okay."

"Goodbye, Tristan," she says, then smiles as she walks away.

CHAPTER
Twenty-Seven

$\mathcal{B}$eing in a car accident royally sucks, but Becca can say with absolute certainty that even with all the aches and pains and the incredibly tiresome cast she's got to lug around on her leg for the next few weeks, the absolute worst part about it is being stuck in her apartment for weeks on end. New York in the dead of winter is not exactly a great place to be when you're on crutches, so for her safety and the safety of those around her, Becca really only leaves her apartment for doctor's appointments, occasional stops at her office, and a couple of dinner dates that Tristan managed to talk her into (including a surprisingly pleasant one with his parents).

Becca has to admit that being homebound for the past month would've been unbearable if it wasn't for Tristan. She was surprised to find out that he's a natural caregiver;

he's incredibly sweet and attentive, and somehow seems to know exactly what Becca needs just before she needs it. That's not to say that they don't bicker occasionally, because they absolutely do. They get over it and move on, and Tristan snuggles up behind her in bed like nothing happened, and it does wonders to quell the small, lingering worry that one day she'll wake up and he'll be gone.

Even though Becca told Tristan before Christmas that she wanted to take it slow, they're pretty much living together now. Tristan hasn't spent the night at his place since her mother left to go back to Ohio, even though she's pretty sure he sneaks over there every few days for some alone time. She's not sure if it's for his sake or for hers, but it's a nice little breather that she's started to look forward to. She's beginning to realize that once she gets her cast off and is able to move around on her own again without needing help from anyone, she doesn't want him to leave. Sure they'll have some logistics to work out, but with three apartments between the two of them, she thinks they'll be able to figure something out.

Becca's sprawled out on her sofa with her leg resting on a pillow, her laptop on her lap and file folders spread out on every available surface when Tristan walks through her front door. He's wearing her favorite suit: well-tailored and navy blue, complete with a red silk tie. He's holding a large paper bag that he sets down on the dining room table before he walks over to her.

"Hi," he says with a grin as he leans down and kisses her. "Busy day?"

"Very. You?"

He nods as he very carefully takes a seat on the sofa next to her. "I sat in on a product development meeting and was actually disappointed when it was over," he says, grinning. It's so nice to see him happy and working on something that he loves and is truly interested in.

Becca laughs. "I wish I had that problem. What's in the bag?"

"Dinner," he replies. "Abby and Cole are coming over tonight, remember?"

Becca sighs, resting her head against the couch cushion. She did *not* remember. "Ugh, I forgot."

"Want me to call and cancel?" Tristan asks, curling a strand of her hair around his finger before it drifts down, outlining the neckline of her shirt and pulling it lower. He leans down and presses a kiss to her collarbone, his whiskers scratching her skin. "We could find something else to do with our time."

"Mmmm," Becca hums. "We could always have them over and then, you know…save that for dessert."

Tristan gives her another kiss, soft and tender, then pulls away. "That sounds like my kind of evening, and…they should be here in fifteen minutes or so. Need help cleaning up?" He nods at the file folders.

"Yes please."

He's got her mess cleaned up in a jiffy, with time left over to cuddle to boot.

Yeah, he can stay.

Becca almost has to laugh at the sight before her: two of the richest men in Manhattan from two of the richest families in the *world* are sitting on her living room floor cross-legged, eating out of half-empty containers of Chinese food. Cole fishes for the last dumpling and eats half, then offers the other half to his wife, feeding her off of his chopsticks. Becca thinks the two of them are as disgustingly adorable as ever. Cole's leaning on one hand, using the free one to eat. Abby's all tucked against his chest, tiny and cute and in love. Tristan's leaning against the sofa where Becca's still laid out, stupid pillow propping up her stupid, aching leg.

"You did a great job with dinner, buddy," Cole says with a grin as he looks across at Tristan.

"Thanks," Tristan replies. "Picked it up myself."

"I'm sure calling in that order was very taxing, babe." Becca slides her fingers through the hair at the nape of Tristan's neck. It's something she started doing after Tristan began working. Seems to relax him.

She catches Abby giving her a soft smile behind the rim of her wine glass (it's filled with cider-Becca can't drink on her meds, so everyone is refraining from the wine tonight). Becca can't even find it in herself to care; she's happy. She wants everyone to know it.

"I was thinking," Cole says, "how do you guys feel about going to the French countryside this summer? My family has a villa there, we could tour the vineyards."

Becca shoots a look at Abby, because that has got to be the most ridiculous sentence anyone has ever uttered in her apartment, and Abby knows it. She gives her friend a look that says, 'Get used to it.'

Tristan turns and grins at her, because he knows what she's thinking, too. He reaches up and puts his hand on her thigh. "If Becca wants."

Oh, Becca wants. "I've never been to Europe before," she says sheepishly.

Tristan squeezes her knee. "I'll take you."

When he looks at her, they have a private conversation: *On the jet, where we'll do stuff,* is what he says.

"Yes please," she replies. To all of it.

Cole drains what's left of his glass and stands. "I've got an early meeting tomorrow, but Tristan and I will get this cleaned up."

Tristan stands and starts picking up containers, and when Cole and Tristan are in the kitchen, Abby takes a seat beside Becca.

"How's the leg?"

"Better. Not the same. Three more weeks until I might get the cast off."

"We'll make a countdown clock and throw a party," Abby says, laughing.

"A pants required party, because of the atrophy. No one wants to see me walking around with one leg that's half the size of the other."

Abby shrugs. "Atrophy schmatrophy. Your legs are cute, especially when they work."

Becca grins and looks up at Tristan when he walks back into the room, her smile growing wider. She can't help it.

"I brought you some water and your pills," he says, dropping them into her open palm.

"Thanks," she says before he leans down and gives her a peck. He waggles his eyebrows at Abby before he picks up the remaining containers.

"You've got yourself a good one," she says.

"Yep." Becca absolutely cannot argue against that. It's a fact.

"And you're happy."

"Abs," she sighs dreamily. "You have no idea how much."

CHAPTER
Twenty-Eight

Cole is smirking at Tristan when he walks back into the kitchen after handing Becca her pills.

"You look like an asshole," Tristan says. "You should stop."

Cole laughs as he puts the leftover moo shu pork in the fridge. "I never thought I'd see you like this," he says.

"Like what?" Cole tosses a wash cloth in the sink as he washes the last of the forks. "And if you say whipped, I will fight you."

"No," Cole says quietly. "All domestic and caring. A good boyfriend. I never thought I'd see it."

"Well," Tristan says, dramatically spreading his arms. "Take a good look."

"Becca's good for you. And you're good to her."

Tristan can't think of a smartass response to that one,

because it's the truth. "I know it's fast," he says, "but she's the one."

Cole grins and claps his friend on the shoulder. "When you know, you know."

Tristan? He *knows.*

"Things are going well with your dad?"

Tristan nods. "They're...better. He's him, you know? But I'm on the right track, finally doing something that I'm interested in."

"You'll be running Blackwell Tech yet," Cole says. He's clearly joking, but Tristan isn't ruling it out anymore, now that the pressure's off.

Maybe someday.

For now, this is enough.

"Lift up," Tristan says, tapping on Becca's right knee. She's sitting at the end of the bed, and Tristan's kneeling on the floor, holding up a huge fuzzy pink sock.

"What are you doing?"

He looks up at her, eyebrow raised. "Helping you put on your socks."

"No," Becca sighs. "I know that, but what's *that*?" She points at the sock in his hand. It looks more like a legging.

"Oh," he replies, gently lifting Becca's cast. "You said your toes were getting cold and I couldn't figure out a way to get a sock over your cast, so I had this made for you."

He slides the sock on, smiling all the while because this thing looks incredibly ridiculous. Becca wiggles her toes and Tristan cups them with his hands and slides his palms back and forth to warm them up.

"That better?" he asks.

When he doesn't hear a response, he looks at Becca who's just sitting there with this beautiful grin and tears in her eyes. "What's-"

"I love you," she says as she runs her fingers along the curve of his jaw.

"What?" Tristan replies, completely dumbfounded. Of all the times he imagined hearing the sentiment, he was never kneeling on the floor in front of her trying to warm up her toes. But it's perfect in its unexpectedness.

Becca laughs, then leans down and kisses him. She says, "I love you," against his lips, and he thinks that might be the perfect way to hear those three perfect words.

"And I love you," he replies, because it's such a nice thing to hear. He wants Becca to hear it from him as often as she can.

"I know." She runs her fingers through his hair. "I've never been with a man who cared so much about my cold toes before."

"I care about all of you," he says, grinning. "Even the cold parts."

Becca grabs his t-shirt and twists, pulling him up to her level and gives him a long, deep kiss, her tongue tangling with his. When she pulls away, she's grinning, and *fuck*, he's hard for her already.

"Take it off," she says, nodding at his shirt.

"Yeah?" He wants to make sure that *she's* sure because since her accident their physical activity has been somewhat limited. They've fooled around a few times so neither one of them has been left completely wanting, but sex is remarkably unsexy when you have to worry about broken ribs and bruises and a bad leg. Positions are a logistical nightmare.

Still, he's aching for her. He misses being inside of her, misses the way her soft skin feels against his when they're moving together.

Becca nods enthusiastically, helping Tristan lift his shirt over his head, like she can't get her hands on his skin quickly enough. "I was promised dessert, and I intend to have it."

Tristan laughs and stands up, removing his pants and boxer briefs, sliding them down to the floor before kicking them off.

Becca lets out this little hum of satisfaction as she looks at him, then she reaches out and strokes his cock, biting her lip as she gives him a coy grin.

It's almost too much to take—her looking at him like that as she slides her hand up and down his length, and he's so wound up that if he's not careful, he's going to come way too soon. He pulls away, leans down and picks her up so he can place her further up on the bed. Halfway there she starts sucking on this spot on his neck that she knows he likes, biting and laving it with her tongue, and he stops for a moment just to enjoy the sensation.

"I thought that might make you drop me," she says huskily in his ear, making him shiver.

He turns his head and plants a kiss on her lips. "I'd never drop you."

Tristan lays her gently on the pillows, careful not to jostle any of her injuries that might still be tender. He reaches over and slides off Becca's panties as she undoes the buttons on the dress shirt of his that she slipped on once he changed out of it earlier this evening.

"Keep the shirt on," he says gruffly.

She teasingly slips a button through its hole. "Like, how *on* are we talking? This on?" She slips her hand under the placket and slides it back far enough so he can see her breast.

"More off is okay," he breathes.

When he can see her other breast, he nods. "That kind of on."

Tristan kneels on the bed and carefully settles himself between Becca's wide-open legs. "You okay?" he asks.

"Mmmm," she hums, kissing her way down his neck.

His mouth meets hers in a hungry kiss that's all lips and teeth and tongue, and then kisses a path that will lead him right between her thighs. "Lie back," he tells her. He's going to be gentle tonight.

"What are you doing?"

Before he answers, Tristan licks one nipple and drags it between his teeth. "I'm going to eat you out," he says, then sucks her other nipple into his mouth. "That okay?"

Her breath hitches before she lets out a ragged, "Yes."

"Good." He moves further down, rubbing his stubble across the soft skin of her belly as she grips his hair. When she trembles, he can't help but feel triumphant.

He slides his hands along the insides of her thighs, loving the way the goosebumps bloom across her skin. She's so wet for him, he can already see it, and he doesn't want to make her wait. He teases her a little, kissing and licking as her back arches off the bed. She slides her hand back behind his head, pulling him closer, and he wraps his arms around the backs of her legs, holding her steady against his mouth. He wants to see how long it takes him to get her off with just his tongue tonight.

He drags the flat of his tongue up her slit, lets it slip inside her before dragging the tip of it along the underside of her clit. Becca tenses immediately, and Tristan looks up to make sure he hasn't-

"Don't stop!" she cries, and he can't help but laugh, which apparently feels good to her, too. He licks and teases her, sucking on her clit before flicking it, gently scraping the most sensitive side with the edge of his teeth before sucking it into his mouth and working it with his tongue the way he knows drives her crazy. Her breathing is out of control, hands fisted in his hair, and she's alternating between these breathy little moans and cries of "Faster, please. More."

Anything she wants, he'll give to her, and before he knows it she's falling apart, muscles contracting as his name falls from her lips.

He kisses his way back up to her, and when he's close enough, her hungry mouth is on his, tasting herself on it. It's so fucking hot the way she does that; he's never been with anyone who was into it before.

"C'mere," she says, and Tristan's surprised to see that

she's already unwrapped a condom.

He moves up so she can reach him, and she slides it down slowly, torturing him while she can. Then he lowers himself down, arms braced on either side of her head. "Tell me if I hurt you, okay?" He's going to do his best not to put any of his weight on her, but he just wants to make sure she'll tell him.

"You won't hurt me," she says with a kiss.

He doesn't see how he could. Tonight he wants it soft and slow as he's cradled in the warmth of her body. But still… "Promise me."

She kisses the tip of his nose, and a wave of affection hits him square in the chest. "I promise."

Tristan slides into Becc and drops his head to her shoulder, overcome with feeling. He rocks into her, and she stretches out, planting her hands against the headboard to give herself leverage so she can meet him thrust for thrust. He latches onto her neck, sucking so hard he hopes he leaves his mark on her, and her hands trace the planes of his back before tangling in his hair.

They whisper "I love yous" as they kiss and touch and move, soft and sweet with the tender passion that's lit by the fire of two people who have had to wait too long to enjoy each other's bodies this way.

Tristan lifts his head to see Becca smiling at him. He smiles back, then leans in close and says, "Touch yourself for me," before going back to work on his favorite spot on her neck.

"Keep doing that," she moans.

He does. He keeps doing that *so* much, until he can feel her tightening around him and all the feeling in his world condenses into one concentrated spot of pleasure growing at the base of his spine, threatening to send him spiraling out of control.

Tristan licks the pad of his thumb, then reaches down and goes to work on Becca's clit, taking over for her so she can fully enjoy this. He sets off a devastating orgasm that pulls him right into his own with a white-hot force that makes his eyes squeeze shut as they both ride it out together.

When he finally pulls out, Becca has this dissatisfied moue that makes him smile. He's not away for long though, just long enough to get her settled on her side beneath the covers. When he gets in the bed behind her, she pushes herself back into his chest, then pulls his arm across her waist, twining her fingers between his. She rests her head on his bicep, and turns her head to the side so he can give her a kiss.

"I love you," she says.

Tristan smiles like the lovesick idiot he is, because he doesn't think he'll ever get tired of hearing those words.

"I love you, too."

"You're staying," she sighs.

It's almost more of a demand than a question, and he knows she's not just talking about tonight.

He nuzzles her neck and breathes in the comforting fruity smell of her shampoo.

"I'm staying."

Epilogue

"*You're* up for a promotion," Becca says, shaking her head. "Isn't that amazing?"

Tristan pulls her closer against him, every inch of his chest pressed against her back. She thinks it might be one of the best feelings in the world, being safe in his arms. They're all sprawled out on a blanket on the beach. The breeze blows through her hair, and she breathes in the salty smell of it.

Tristan rests his chin on her shoulder and says, "Amazing because I'm still employed and apparently promotable, or..."

"Amazing because you're smart and you work hard and you're going to get rewarded for it." She slides her hand across his forearm, letting him know that she gets that he's used to being self-deprecating, but she's not letting him get away with it this time.

"This wine is really good, by the way. Excellent choice."

Becca nods, then swallows what little is left in her glass. "I do know how to pick 'em."

"Our next place needs to have a wine cellar," Tristan says.

"Our *next* place? We just moved into our current place." Their current place being Tristan's "grown-up" apartment with the great view. They decorated it together, so it's completely *theirs*, although Becca insisted Tristan bring along the fluffy, comfy furniture.

"Just planning ahead. Apparently that's a big thing in the business world. I'm learning a lot about it."

Becca laughs and slaps Tristan's knee. "Smartass. Question?"

"Answer," Tristan replies.

"Not that I'm questioning your decision-making skills or anything, and this truly has been a lovely evening," she says, reaching out for his hand. "But if you're so big into planning now, then why did you think it was a good idea to bring me back to Cole's family's beach house? Do they even know we're here?"

Cole and Abby are in Europe celebrating their anniversary, and Becca and Tristan are going to join them in two days. She hopes they make it and don't get arrested for trespassing.

"Yes," Tristan replies with a laugh. "They know we're here. I have the keys to the house."

"Okay." Becca relaxes. "That's good."

Tristan kisses her neck a few times, in that spot he knows makes her weak. "Remember the night we spent out here?"

"When we met? Of course." She tries not to think about

it that much, even though they've moved on.

"We sat like this, and I kissed your neck like this…"

Ugh, he's doing it again. She's so weak for him, it's totally unfair.

"I remember," she says, laying her arms over his where they wrap around her waist and hugging him close.

"Do you remember what we talked about that night?"

"Constellations," Becca breathes, a little distracted.

"I had no idea what I was talking about." He nibbles along the slope of her shoulder, like the bastard he is.

"I know." Her breath catches and she smiles. "But I didn't care about that because you were doing…*ungh*…that."

He lets out a laugh across the wet mark his tongue left on her skin, and she shivers.

"I wanted you to keep doing that," she tells him, "and then you…"

"I left."

"Yeah," she says regretfully. "So why you'd bring us back here after that, I don't know. This place doesn't exactly hold good memories for us."

"I wanted to change that," he says.

"You're doing a good job."

"Becca," he says with a hitch in his voice that makes Becca turn around.

God, he looks…he almost looks nervous. "Are you okay?" She's panicking a little.

"C'mere," he says, placing his hand on her hips and turning her until she's facing him, her knees on either side of his thighs. "How's the leg."

"Bendy," she replies. "Perfect. Pain-free."

"Good." He presses a soft kiss to her lips.

She cups his jaw and slides her thumb across his cheek. "What's the matter?"

He grins at her, and even here at sunset it's brighter than the sun. "Nothing. Everything's perfect."

"Oh…kay."

"I brought you here because I thought it would be romantic."

Okay, she'll bite. "Romantic how?"

He slides his hands along the small of her back, pulling her closer. "I thought it would be romantic for me to bring you back to the place I ran away from committing to you, to ask you if you would commit to me."

Becca thinks her heart might be ready to beat right out of her chest. "Tristan, what?"

"I love you," he says, searching her eyes.

"I love *you*," Becca replies.

"You've changed my life, and I could never repay you for all the things you've given me, but I want to try. I'll try for the rest of my life if you'll let me."

She feels his hands slip away from her waist, and next thing she knows, he's holding a black velvet box with a ring in it. She only looks at it for a second before her gaze drifts back to his. Tristan leans forward and kisses her long and slow.

When they part, he rests his forehead against hers. "Marry me," he whispers.

He pulls the ring out of the box and slides it on her

trembling finger. It's absolutely gorgeous, and exactly the ring she'd pick out if she had every one on earth to choose from: an antique art deco ring, in a simple platinum setting with small, delicate diamonds stretching across the band.

"Oh my god," Becca says. "Tristan."

"It belonged to my grandmother," he tells her, sliding the tip of his thumb just above the diamond. "She and my grandfather were married for seventy years. I want seventy more."

She smiles through her tears because she wants that too. She wants it more than anything else in this world.

"Please," he says, smiling. "Marry me." He presses a kiss to her lips. "Please say yes."

That's exactly what she does.

About the Author

Cassie Cross is a Maryland native and a romantic at heart, who lives outside of Baltimore with her two dogs and a closet full of shoes. Cassie's fondness for swoon-worthy men and strong women are the inspiration for most of her stories, and when she's not busy writing a book, you'll probably find her eating takeout and indulging in her love of 80's sitcoms.

Cassie loves hearing from her readers, so please follow her on Twitter (@ CrossWrites) or leave a review for this book on the site you purchased it from. Thank you!

Printed in Great Britain
by Amazon